Lock Down Publications and Ca$h
Presents

LAND OF DA

HOOLIGANZ

Can't Stop, Won't Stop
PART 4

Written By
IRA B

First Edition 2025

Printed in the United States of America

This is a work of fiction. Names, characters, places, and incidents either are products of the author's imagination or are used fictitiously. Any similarity to actual events or locales or persons, living or dead, is entirely coincidental.

Lock Down Publications
P.O. Box 944
Stockbridge, GA 30281
www.lockdownpublications.com

Like our page on Facebook: Lock Down Publications
www.facebook.com/lockdownpublications.ldp

Stay Connected with Us!

Text **LOCKDOWN** to 22828 to stay up-to-date with new releases, sneak peaks, contests and more…

Like our page on Facebook:
Lock Down Publications

Join Lock Down Publications/The New Era Reading Group

Visit our website:
www.lockdownpublications.com

Follow us on Instagram:
Lock Down Publications

Email Us: We want to hear from you!

Acknowledgments

To the big homie, Walt Holmes, I hope you are keeping your head up behind da wall. We miss your realness, my nigga. Stay true and know that it's all love on this side.

Next in line is the beautiful duo, Kiana and Niecey, my beautiful god sisters, whom I want to apologize to for not spending much time with you growing up. But I still love you and hope one day I can make it up to you. You'll always have that special place in my heart.

Last, but not least, I love you Keylijah, like only a big brother should. Sorry I'm not there for you, brah, but eventually these gates will open and set me free. When that day comes, we gonna ball! We gon' live it up like I never left! Keep it player, lil brah. Peace.

DEDICATION

This one is for you, my dear beloved haters, who spoke negatively of me and said I'd never amount to anything. But look at me now. I'm a unique storyteller, who plans on stopping no time soon. So, sit back and watch me do much greater things with my God-given gift, as a writer. I truly appreciate the motivation.

Chapter 1

When Taquan exited the house with the bag of loot he was given by Da'Jhana, he quietly confronted his emotions regarding where his relationship stood with her all this time. Her love for him still remained firm, despite all the bullshit they had gone through together. Taquan wasn't even surprised when she produced what was left of the lick Boozy had hit before he died, a lick from which Souljah called himself trying to intimidate Da'Jhana into giving up the loot. She held firm, and Taquan saluted her on that. She wasn't one, by far, to be easily intimidated.

As for Souljah, the nigga was grimy, so much so, that Taquan felt the need to intervene. At any given time, Souljah would find his way back to collect that loot, and this time, Da'Jhana probably wouldn't be able to survive.

That's why Taquan was taking it upon himself to confront Souljah about it and see what he had on his mind. All it took was one false move, and blood would be spilled.

There was no room for bullshittin'.

When Taquan got back inside the car, he tossed the backpack on the floor behind him. Then the sound of his new cell phone rang and Taquan took his time retrieving it from his front pocket. When he recognized Bred Man's name on the display, he hurriedly answered the call, without further hesitation.

"So that's how we playin', my nigga?" said Bred Man.

"What?" he replied humbly.

"You know what, brah. You left the spot without lettin' us know you was gone. We was out here lookin' all over for you, my nigga. You good?" Bred Man was the closer to Taquan than the others, but they all loved and respected one another equally.

"Had some shit to take care of," said Taquan.

"But you good though?"

Taquan nodded his head in answer, but what came from his mouth next was something totally different. "Naw, my nigga. I ain't good at all. I might have to take it there with a nigga in a minute."

"Who?"

"Souljah," he said.

"What he do?" Bred Man asked.

It was a brief moment before Taquan answered, and when he did, he said. "Meet me over at Dreka's crib and I'll lace you up on everything there. I'm on my way over there right now."

"Say no more," said Bred Man.

When he disconnected, Taquan started up the car and put it in gear. Before taking off, he took one more glance over at the house. From the living room window, he noticed the curtains move, which was all the evidence he needed to know that Da'Jhana was checking for him.

With a brief nod, Taquan sped away from the curb, heading for his sister Dreka's house. By now, the block party was in full swing, and here he was in the streets lurking and looking for trouble.

It didn't take him long to reach Dreka's house over in the Shaw Quarter's community. He parked the car in the driveway of a white brick house that was in serious need of a pressure wash. Also occupying the driveway was his sister's 2018 Lexus LC 500 that he bought her for her 25th birthday, several months ago. He parked the car behind the Lexus, retrieved the backpack and got out and headed for the front door of the house. This was where Taquan was going to be staying until he got back on his feet properly.

Bred Man hadn't made it there yet, so Taquan decided to go on inside and put away the loot till he arrived. Then they would get down to business, where the fate of Souljah stood in the balance.

Inside the house, Dreka was in the process of getting dressed in her bedroom, which was across the hall from the guest room he would be claiming as his own. Taquan glanced in the open doorway of his sister's room and saw that she was half naked. Dreka and her 42-inch ass was all over the place. Taquan frowned in disgust, slamming her bedroom door shut and ducking off into his own room. She shouted some bullshit after him about privacy in her own house, but Taquan paid her no mind and proceeded doing what he came to do. He stashed the loot and prepare for the confrontation he was about to have with Souljah.

Ten minutes later, Bred Man came knocking, accompanied by Duke, Todd, and Brewski, who was Bred Man's older cousin that he managed to cop a ride from. When Taquan stepped outside on the front porch amongst them, he automatically knew things were not about to go right with Duke being present. He and Souljah were cousins, and Duke looked up to his big cousin, which just might be a problem they didn't need right now.

Brewski was just there to support Bred Man, but Taquan felt he could be of good use for the mission.

Taquan approached Duke and looked him dead in the eyes. "What I'm about to say and do has nothing to do with you, personally. But it does have a personal interest regarding your cousin, Souljah. So, before I go any further with what I have to say, I'm giving you the option to walk away and have nothing to do wit' what's about to happen."

"What Souljah do?" asked Duke

"Just know that he crossed someone I love dearly."

"Are you gonna kill him?"

Bred Man looked over at him quietly, as if he was anticipating Duke to say some slick shit.

Taquan said, "I'm giving you the option to walk away now, Duke. Walk away and don't intervene, unless it's to assist HCG on this mission."

"I can't go against my own blood, brah," said Duke.

"Then walk away," said Bred Man.

Duke looked at him like he was crazy. Then Taquan placed a hand on his shoulder.

"The game ain't based on sympathy, Duke. You make your choice. Go. But," said Taquan with a hardened facial expression, "if you so ever intervene in this business to try and save your cousin, then you may as well consider yourself the enemy as well," he expressed.

"So, it's like that?" said Duke

"You've been given an option, Duke." Taquan was not the type to back down from anything or anyone.

With the shake of his head, Duke turned around and walked away. He didn't even look back, as he separated himself from the rest of the crew.

After watching him distance himself from them, Bred Man turned his gaze on Taquan and was about to say something before Taquan cut him off.

"I don't wanna hear it, Bred Man," he said. "You know damn well you shouldn't have brought him here, when I already told you what the deal was."

"I wasn't thinkin', my nigga. That's my bad."

"Fuckin' right, it's your bad," Taquan snapped at him. "Now, we might have to knock his black ass off, too, brah!"

All Bred Man could do was shake his head. He had fucked up.

"Let's get down to it." said Taquan. Then he got down to business and dared Bred Man not to fuck this up, too.

Chapter 2

Back at the hospital, White Boy Ty couldn't believe his eyes, as he stared into the back of the car at the crying child. He released his grip from around Shamoorah's throat and leaned into the passenger window to stare at the little girl. So beautiful she was, with a pair of blue eyes that White Boy Ty knew without a shadow of a doubt mirrored his own. The child was the spitting image of him, and as he stared at her crying her poor little heart out, Ty glanced over at Shamoorah with the most menacing look he could muster.

"What's going on, Ty?" asked Jamir, having been thrown off guard by the sudden act of domestic violence. Without saying a word, White Boy Ty opened the rear passenger door of the car and slid into the backseat next to the crying child.

"I'm sorry, Jamir," said Shamoorah.

"I'm lost like a muthafucker," he replied, looking from her, back to his brother, then the little girl that he could now see favored White Boy Ty. Jamir was at a loss for words, as he watched his brother unbuckle the child from her car seat and lift her up into his embrace like it was the natural thing to do.

"Shamoorah," said White Boy Ty in a serious tone of voice. "Get your ass in this car, now!" Then he saw the female sitting behind the wheel of the car staring back at him in alarm.

Without having to be told twice, Shamoorah shot Jamir another apologetic glance and climbed back into the front passenger seat. If looks could kill, the way Ty was glaring at her that very moment, she would be dead, or soon to be if she tested his patience farther.

"What's the play, big brah?" Jamir asked

"I'll hit your line when I'm done," said White Boy Ty, then he gave Shamoorah the signal that he was ready to get a move on. "I'm ready," he announced.

"You can go now, Abigail," said Shamoorah. "We good," she sighed, refusing to look back at White Boy Ty.

"Naw," said Ty, frowning, "we ain't good."

When the car started rolling, Jamir ordered two of his men to follow Ty and make sure he was safe, while in traffic. They did as they were told and were tailing the car minutes later, as they rode towards the heart of town.

For a long moment, the car was quiet between the adults, as White Boy Ty awkwardly managed to finesse the child into silence. It was a small relief, but the rage inside his heart was still loud and threatening to explode at any given moment. It was one thing for Shamoorah to cross him on some selfish, greed shit, like she did before. But this was on a whole other level. A child was involved now, one that was his all this time, and he didn't even know it until just now. Ty had a right to be pissed at her. He wanted to snap her fuckin' neck.

"Where are we going?" asked Abigail. She was a cross between black and Caucasian, pretty but plumped, and borderline offensive by her potent body odor.

"Who the hell are you?' asked White Boy Ty. He had the child nestled in the crook of his arm, while offering her his big Jesus piece medallion to play with. Baby girl was marveling over its numerous diamonds.

"She's a good friend of mine that I've known for years, growing up back home," said Shamoorah.

"I'm guessing you lied about that, too, huh?" Ty replied with a hint of annoyance.

Shamoorah shrugged her shoulders and let out a frustrated breath, while rubbing her throat gently, where he had been in the process of choking her out. Good thing the child intervened or shit would have gotten drastic.

"What I told you about my life and where I'm from was the truth, Ty. And I'm still not going back home to those people," said Shamoorah.

"Whatever, Shamoorah," he adjusted himself in the backseat and stared down at the little girl, who was now looking up at him curiously. "What's her name?" asked White Boy Ty.

"Nikita Naomi," she said.

"Nikita," he muttered, and ran a finger over her nose. She giggled at that. Ty allowed himself a small smile and just pulled the child closer.

"She's eleven months old, Ty. She's the best thing to ever happen to me, and I have you to thank for that. Because of you and her, I now have a new perspective in life. That scared little girl you once knew is dead and gone now, Ty. I'm a woman now, a mother, and I have so much more in life to offer than all the bullshit I was carrying around with me, when we first met." Shamoorah had turned around in her seat to face him.

At first, Ty couldn't stand the likes of her, but after hearing her out and seeing the change in her attitude, he now regarded Shamoorah in a whole new light.

"Then why did it take you this long to show up?" said White Boy Ty.

"Because I had to focus on gettin' myself right first, Ty," she replied.

"And then by lying to my little brotha, manipulating him into believing you're somebody you not, just to use him to get to me?" he replied

"Rather you believe it or not, Ty, I didn't even know Jamir was connected to you, until just now. When I was down in Tampa, building a life with our daughter, I saw on the news what was going on up here. Then I remembered you telling me this was where you was from. I was scared for you, Ty. Really, I was. Then I said fuck it, lemme come up here and see if I can reach you somehow. I didn't know what I was doing, Ty. All I know was being here, somehow I could find some type of connection to reach you. I didn't think it was through Jamir. I met him just recently, in the parking lot of a restaurant. We clicked and we kept in touch, but only on some legitimate stuff. I know all about his girl and his kid, but never once did he mention anything regarding you, nor did I ask. But, yet it turns out that God has led me to you through him anyway. And now that you are here," said Shamoorah, turning away from Ty, as though ashamed over something she wanted to say, but couldn't quite get it out.

"Now that I'm here, what?" said White Boy Ty, seeing that she was having difficulty saying what was really on her mind now.

"Nothing," she ducked her head and sighed. "Welcome to fatherhood," she said quietly.

White Boy Ty could pretty much understand what was going through her mind at that point. What she did to him before shouldn't matter now, because what's more important was the young life they now shared as parents. But Ty would never forget how clever and dangerous Shamoorah was when she needed to be. Regardless of the things she said and her new outlook on life, she definitely was not the person to sleep on. Shamoorah was just as ruthless as he was a young goon in his prime.

a father was something he had always thought about being one day. But not like this, not in the middle of such chaos. Then there was Toby and her situation to think about. She too was pregnant with his child, and White Boy Ty didn't know whether that child was still safe or not.

When he learned of Toby's pregnancy, Ty didn't know how to feel about that. He didn't know whether he should be happy or scared. Although he knew Toby would do everything in her power to protect the seed that was growing in her womb, it still scared Ty shitless to know that something bad could happen at any time during her incarceration. That was a fear in itself that was eating Ty alive inside.

Losing Toby was one thing, but losing their unborn child in the process was pain that White Boy Ty wasn't sure he could endure.

Could Shamoorah and Nikita's presence be some type of omen? wondered Ty. Was God trying to tell him something in a way of their existence?

"I'm still scared, Ty," said Shamoorah, snatching him out of his disturbing thoughts.

"I am, too," he replied.

Now she was turning back around to face him. "What are you afraid of, Ty? Please tell me, because I've never known you to be afraid of anything," said Shamoorah. Seeming surprised, all of a sudden.

"Then you don't know me at all," Ty said.

"Make me know you," she persisted.

So he did. He told her all about Toby and how much she meant to him. Then he went on to tell her where they stood now, which to his surprise, Shamoorah accepted her faults and respected his mind, and from there a mutual understanding was set in place. Ty would be a fool to miss out on being a father to his child. But there still was so much that needed to be done in order for him to fully take on the responsibility as a father. Most of that had everything to do with Toby and his position in the HCG crew. He had a decision to make. Life was giving him an ultimatum, and he better choose wisely.

Chapter 3

As he put distance between him and the others, Duke was wrestling with the decision of what he needed to do. What Taquan had in mind to do to Souljah, he wanted no parts in that. Souljah was family. He was something like that big brother he never had.

What Duke didn't understand was why bother bringing him along to discuss Souljah's fate, when they knew he wouldn't go against his own family. *Do they think that low of me?* thought Duke.

He would take Souljah's side whether he was wrong or right. Duke wouldn't be able to live with himself if he assisted his crew in harming the only family he had left that meant something to him.

Duke was fifteen years old, but he was far from stupid. If Taquan and the rest thought he was not loyal to his own, then they had another thing coming. He knew he was now being looked on as a traitor. He could literally feel the dark stares from Taquan and the others boring into his back as he walked away. Although he had been given a choice to decide whether he was siding with the crew regarding Souljah's fate, it still didn't feel fair to Duke to have to choose family over his blood family. But now that he had chosen, Duke knew that he had to warn his cousin before it went down.

Before he even realized where he was at, Duke had found himself standing alongside the Shaw Quarter Stop gas station with his phone in hand. He had made it all the way back up to the entrance of the neighborhood. There he contemplated whether he should call Souljah to warn him about Taquan and his plan to see about him.

"Duke?" A voice interrupted his thought process.

Duke looked up at the sound of his name and saw two girls having rounded the corner of the neighborhood store. Both girls he knew as Kariah and Alyssa.

"When you get out, Duke?" asked Kariah. She was a young, tender sixteen year old cut yellow bone something, with pink braces on her teeth and well-proportioned like a grown woman.

"Got out today," he answered.

"You done got big and stuff, too," she added.

Duke absently flexed his biceps and shrugged his shoulders with nonchalance. Alyssa, also cute and full-figured, rolled her eyes, giving her undivided attention to the bag of Cool Ranch Doritos in her possession.

"Did Man get out, too?" asked Alyssa, who obviously had no interest in Duke at all.

"Yeah. The whole crew home. They throwin' a big welcome home block party for us back in the hood."

"For real?"

Duke nodded, "Yep."

"Then why you ain't there?"

"Because time is money, Kariah. Don't got time for partyin' right now. I'll holla at y'all some other time, though," he said. Then Duke turned away from them to proceed calling his cousin.

Behind him, both girls gave each other a high five, saying how they were about to go check out the block party. They hurried off in search of someone to give them a ride over to Pepper Hill, where it was going down.

"What?" came the reply when Souljah's phone was answered, but it wasn't by him.

16

Mia, Duke thought to himself, knowing no female would be answering his cousin's phone other than Mia McNeil herself. This was Souljah's on and off girlfriend.

"What's up, Mia? This Duke. Where cuz at?" he replied, stepping around the front of the store.

"His black ass right here," she snapped.

After what sounded like the phone being thrown at him, Souljah's voice came over the line moments later, and he didn't sound like he was up for conversation.

"We got a problem, cuz," said Duke.

Souljah let out a frustrated breath. "That's my fault, lil cuz. I know I shoulda been there to see you come home. I got tied up with some business."

"I don't care about that shit, Souljah. We need to talk. Some shit is about to go down and you need to know what's going on."

"What the fuck you talkin' bout, Duke?'

"Where you at right now, cuz?"

"Where you at?" Souljah asked.

Duke told him where he was. When Souljah said he would be there in a few minutes, Duke assured him that he would be there waiting.

About six minutes later, Duke was posted up outside the front of the store, downing a bottle of Gatorade, when Souljah pulled up in a navy-blue Cadillac Escalade truck, sitting nice on 30-inch face rims. The SUV came to a stop in front of Duke. The front passenger window rolled down to reveal not only Souljah but Mia occupying the truck as well.

"What the hell you waitin' on, cuz? Get in," said Souljah, leaning across Mia's lap.

When Duke hopped in the back behind Mia, he was then passed a fresh lit blunt of Runtz by his cousin. Without hesitation, Duke hit the blunt and allowed the weed smoke to calm his nerves.

"Now what's so important that you need to tell me, cuz?" Souljah questioned.

After hitting the blunt a few more times, Duke passed it back up front. Mia took it and put the blunt to her luscious lips next.

"I don't know what's going on, but Taquan is plottin' somethin'," Duke stated, as he lounged back in his seat.

"Something like what?" asked Souljah

"Whatever reason you gave him to want to come after you."

"Me?" Souljah was obviously baffled by this revelation.

Duke nodded. "He said you crossed him."

"Hmph." Mia blew smoke from her nose.

Souljah looked over at her and frowned. "We'll discuss this shit further, after I drop Mia off," he said, and Mia just rolled her eyes.

During the next twelve minutes, riding to the Wal-Mart shopping center, where Mia worked as a manager, the two cousins conducted small talk and avoided talking about street shit in her presence. Mia got out, wearing her feelings on her sleeve. She didn't even acknowledge Souljah in parting ways, only slammed the door in her wake.

"What's wrong wit her?" asked Duke, after claiming the front passenger seat.

"Everything." Souljah pulled off, heading back to get in traffic. "So, your lil hooligan brotha wanna see me, huh?" he chuckled.

"I wonder why."

"I know why he do."

"Why?"

Souljah stroked his goatee as he nosed the front of his truck into moving traffic, along the main highway leading back towards town.

"There's only one thang I can think of, and I know it's about that bitch!"

"What bitch?"

"Da'Jhana?"

"Da'Jhana?" said Duke. The look he gave his cousin was one of absolute puzzlement. "What do she gotta do with anythang?"

The big SUV swerved into traffic, barely missing another truck by at least a foot and a half. After nearly causing a major vehicular accident, Souljah floored the truck toward the High Bridge area and took to the back streets, until he made it to his next destination back over in Joy Land. There he parked the Cadillac Escalade in the garage and phoned one of his Bully Gang affiliates to reserve him a stolen car to roll in.

"From now on, Duke, that HCG shit is dead. I shoulda never let you get down wit them clown ass niggaz anyway." They were now standing in the front yard of the house.

It was Jamir who had recruited Duke. Now this situation would put them at odds. To go up against him was the last thing Duke wanted. But Taquan left him no other choice.

"So that means you puttin me on wit' Bully Gang, then?" asked Duke.

"Listen, cuz, you don't need no gang to define who you are. Be your own man. That's how you get respected more, lil cuz. You've put in more work by yourself than a lot of them clowns. But if Bully Gang is what you want now, I'ma have to take you up before the board members first. That's protocol, lil cuz," said Souljah.

"A'ight," Duke was all for that.

"But only after you complete this mission."

"What mission?"

Souljah grinned that devilish grin of his. Duke knew that look, and it only meant trouble. The last time he saw that grin somebody lost their teeth and ended up with brain damage.

Soon after, Bully Rell pulled up in a black Dodge Magnum and both Duke and Souljah got in. "That was quicker than I expected," said Souljah. He got into the front passenger seat. Duke slid in behind him and remained quiet.

"This is what I do," said Bully Rell.

"Facts."

"Where we headed?"

When Souljah answered his question, it made Duke do a double take. Souljah wanted to set an example, and that example regarded the fate of none other than Da'Jhana. It was her who had brought them to this point, and for that she was about to be dealt with accordingly.

Then Taquan would be forced to move right into his trap.

"And I want you to knock this hoe muthafuckin' head off, too," said Souljah to his cousin.

Duke just looked at him in quiet resolve. This was the part he was worried about. This was that fuck shit.

Chapter 4

The instant LJ exited the law office building, after spending quality time with Nancy and convincing her to tell all she knew about Damian, he had a little pep in his step. He headed for his car, but not before scanning his immediate surroundings to see if Damian was still hanging about outside the building. He wasn't, or at least he wasn't visible, like he was before.

Can't sleep on that nigga, thought LJ, as he hopped into the car he'd parked across the street. He knew Damian was not the one to be underestimated, which is why he left Nancy with his backup gun, a compact Browning nine-millimeter, fully loaded, to keep her safe in case the nigga showed his face. Nancy claimed she wasn't a stranger to firearms, she used to go to the gun range with her cousin, Jimmy, who was not only ex-military but an awesome marksman. So, Nancy assured LJ that if any pressure came, it would be from her squeezing the trigger.

Back in the car, LJ hit Delani's new number up and informed him that he had a location. Although the mission to get rid of Damian was his, in exchange for Diva's commitment and her cooperation to be a valuable asset to the crew, LJ still thought it best to acknowledge his superior first.

"Where you at right now? We need to put this play in motion," said LJ.

"You know where Tessey's International Kitchen at?" Delani spoke up in that cool, collected tone of his.

"That's in the Bronx, right?"

Delani confirmed.

"Meet me there," said Delani. "I need to lace you up on what's going on over here anyway."

"Say no more, my nigga."

After hanging up with Delani, he sent a quick text to Shamar to let him know he had a location. Shamar responded quickly, informing him that he was already with Delani. With that being said, LJ got into traffic and headed for the Bronx.

When he reached the food joint, LJ also saw that Shoo Baby was among the crew. If that was the case, then he wondered where Dejah was, because Shoo Baby was something like a shadow to her. They were always close to one another.

"What it do," LJ slid in the table booth next to Shoo Baby, who in turn gave him a bump of the fist in greeting. "What's the play?"

"You first," said Delani.

LJ noticed that Delani was not looking at him but past him, over his shoulder, at something else. He wanted to look back but decided against it, in case Delani had reasons for discretion. So, he told them about his visit with Nancy at the law firm, and how he had to convince her that there's a possibility that her life was in danger.

"The muthafucker was outside her building?" said Shamar.

LJ nodded.

"Good thang it was you, not me." Delani shot a fleeting glance over at LJ. "That nigga woulda been dead right where he stood."

"And your ass would've broke protocol by reacting recklessly, too," noted Shoo Baby.

She was right. All it took was one mishap and their whole cover would be blown. So much for discretion.

Delani didn't even respond, just refocused his attention at whatever it was behind LJ that he could not see but wanted to look so bad.

"But I got a location," said LJ. "Apparently, the nigga got a five year old daughter that lives out in Yonkers. The little girl lives wit' her godparents and their two kids," he added.

"What's up wit the baby mama?"

LJ said, "She's dead. There's talk that she died in a car accident just after the little girl was born. So now she's being raised by her godparents. Nancy thinks there was some foul play involved wit' what happened wit' the baby mama," he replied.

"I don't give a fuck about all that," said Delani.

"Me neither," LJ shrugged.

Right then Dejah appeared at LJ's left. He looked up at her in surprise. Then he instantly rose up out of his seat to offer it to her. But Dejah shook her head no, and told LJ to remain seated. She and Shoo Baby were about to leave.

"What's happening right now?" LJ turned his gaze on Shamar, as Dejah and Shoo Baby headed for the exit, without a backwards glance.

"We just landed us another valuable ally," said Shamar.

"Wit' who?"

"Pepper."

"And who the hell is Pepper?"

This time it was Delani who had spoken. "She's another bitch sis met in prison. But get this," shrugging his shoulders, Delani said, "Our man, Damian, is also responsible for Pepper's brotha catchin' forty years in the Feds. So, our plan to body this nigga would put us in her graces."

"But what does she have to offer?"

"Her uncle, Savage Joe."

"Okay. What's the business wit' him?"

Delani smirked, "Apparently, he's part of the underworld here and has a lot of clout. Supposedly, Savage Joe is tied in wit' the mob and we can capitalize wit' that by doing what we do.

"If that's the case, then why this nigga ain't dead yet? A nigga wit' mob ties-"

"That's just what he is, a nigga wit' mob ties. A nigga of Damian's caliber is a peon to them. Its' really up to us to make it happen."

"Then let's stop talkin' about it and do it. I'm tired of hearing about this clown. Let's just kill the nigga and be done wit' it," said Shamar. He and Delani locked eyes, and the matter was settled.

Delani said, "Let's do it."

Ten minutes later, LJ was back on the road again, after promising to meet up with the crew later. Tonight, they would utilize the information he attained and finally put an end to their troubles.

Meanwhile, his cellphone rang. He retrieved it to see who was calling him. When he saw that it was his cousin, Shane, calling, he frowned and answered the phone hesitantly.

"What I told you about callin' this phone, cuz?" LJ answered agitatedly.

"You said if anythang wit' Hev changes to hit you up immediately," said Shane. "Well it did."

At hearing those words, LJ felt his heart sink. "What is it, cuz?"

"She done finally woke up," he said.

A tear escaped LJ's eyes at that confirmation. "Damn."

That was when everything changed.

Chapter 5

Da'Jhana was across the street at Naomi's house when she saw the black Dodge Magnum drive past. She, Naomi and their homegirl, Quesha, were sitting out on the screened-in front porch, chillin' and gossiping about the latest street news. The Jr. Hooliganz were now home, and a big block party was going on across town.

Quesha and Mane's older sister, Porshia, were close friends, and she wanted to be there at the celebration homecoming party for the Jr. Hooliganz. Word on the streets was the party was lit, even though the younger hooliganz had gradually left the scene to go do whatever it was that demanded their attention.

Da'Jhana laughed at something Naomi said and absentmindedly glanced up the street. The black car was now headed back in the opposite direction after turning around at the end of the street.

When Da'Jhana noticed this a premonition of danger awakened in her. She remembered what Taquan had told her earlier about watching her back and trusting no one. Seeing the car doubling back around made her suspect trouble amiss.

Somebody was lurking.

After a while, the car suddenly lurched to a stop in front of her house. Da'Jhana shot to her feet at once. The front and back passenger doors opened, and two niggas jumped out.

From her vintage point, Da'Jhana would have sworn she saw the trunk of the car pop open in the back.

"Oh shit, Daj," gasped Quesha, who was now up on her feet next.

By this time, the two goons, who were wearing dark shades and hats pulled low over their eyes, were rushing towards the front door of Da'Jhana's house. The thought of her sister Tiwanna being left in the house alone made Da'Jhana panic.

Then they all watched in shock and horror as the front door was kicked in. The two armed goons, one of which Da'Jhana knew to be Souljah, rushed in the house, like a pair of mercenaries. Almost immediately, two gunshots rang out inside the house and Da'Jhana reached for the gun that she tucked in her jacket pocket. She pulled it out just as three more shots exploded from the house. That was all the encouragement Da'Jhana needed to go be there for her big sister.

"No, don't go!" Naomi reached for Da'Jhana's arm when she hurried towards the door.

"Let me go, Naomi. Tiwanna's in there," Da'Jhana yelled and snatched away from her friend. She bound for the screen door, just as she spotted none other than Duke running from her house. Da'Jhana ran towards him as he rushed for the car.

When Duke saw her running in his direction, while clutching her gun, he upped his pistol and sent two shots in her direction.

"Motherfucker," screamed Da'Jhana and ducked from the wild shots Duke sent her way. But she did hear one of them zoom inches past her right ear. Then she aimed her gun and squeezed the trigger.

Duke managed to make it to the car and literally dived in it through the rear passenger window. The black Dodge Magnum roared from the scene. Da'Jhana sent two more shots its way, shattering the car's rear window in the process.

"Fuck," she stomped her foot in frustration.

Tiwanna. Panic and fear rocked her world. Da'Jhana ran for her house.

By this time, the black car was screeching around the corner down the street. The front door of her house was left hanging off one of its hinges. When Da'Jhana entered through the door into the foyer, she found Souljah. He was still alive, but barely holding on. He looked up at her in fear and helplessness as a hole in his chest spewed blood, draining hm of his life force. But Da'Jhana just shook her head sadly and stepped around him.

In the living room, laid out on the floor dead from a gunshot wound to the head is where she found Tiwanna. She had also taken another bullet to the stomach area, as well. Seeing her sister dead made Da'Jhana weak in the knees. Something very dark inside her woke up. Thoughts of losing her brother Broozy, and now her big sister, the one who raised her like only a true mother would, a piece of her died along with them.

That piece was her sanity.

Vengeance is warranted.

Turning around and hurrying back into the foyer, Da'Jhana looked up at the door and saw Naomi and Quesha standing there. Their presence was of little importance, compared to the deadly storm raging in her heart at that very moment.

Souljah knew it though. He saw the murder in her eyes when she turned her gaze upon him.

"You killed my sista," Da'Jhana growled.

Souljah closed his eyes.

Blocka. Blocka. Blocka. Blocka.

That was the sound of the explosions from the gun as Souljah's brains were splattered all over the wall and floor. Naomi shrieked in terror, and Quesha leaned over and vomited everywhere.

"You killed him." Naomi couldn't believe her eyes.

"They killed my sista," said Da'Jhana.

"But what about Duke?"

The instant she heard his name, something else came over her and Da'Jhana turned around and rushed back through the house.

Naomi and Quesha looked at each other. Neither of them knew what to do or say at that point. They had just witnessed their best friend commit murder in cold blood, without even blinking an eye.

A minute later, Da'Jhana came rushing back to the front of the house. Without a word to her friends, she brushed past them, carrying a leather backpack, and headed out the front door.

"Daj?" Quesha called out after her. But Da'Jhana was hearing nothing, except for the sound in her head of her blowing Duke's brains out next.

Tiwanna's burgundy Infiniti was parked in the driveway. Da'Jhana hit the automatic lock on the door and hopped in behind the wheel. Moments later, she was burning rubber backing out of the driveway into the street. Then she peeled out, roaring away from the house in the same fashion the black Dodge Magnum had done, not too long ago.

She was on a murder mission.

Duke had to die.

Chapter 6

The moment Heaven finally opened her eyes, she was hit with an extremely bright white light, so bright that she shut her eyes and groaned in discomfort. That was when she heard her mother's loving voice. "Hev? Heaven? Baby girl? Please tell me you can hear me, baby," came Monica's rush of worlds.

Heaven groaned again.

Right then, the monitor next to Heaven's bed started beeping like crazy. Monica screamed for the doctor, and the whole clinical staff came running.

Once word got out that Heaven had awakened from her coma, her whole team celebrated. Then, all at once, her Royal Mafia team began alerting everybody and waiting in turn to see her. The queen had awakened.

After the doctor did his much needed routine exercises to determine whether Heaven was actually stable or not, he gave the approval of a head nod and took his leave. But not before warning Monica and all the others that Heaven was still in the healing process and not to push her too hard.

Lashonda, Tilly, Jamir, Sheena, LaVetra, and several others were also occupying the room. Everybody was fighting for Heaven's attention, but all she wanted was to see her daughter. That was when Jamir phoned Shamar's wife, Danielle, who was babysitting Heaven's little girl for the time being. Anya was called and said she was on her way as they spoke.

29

"Hold on," said Heaven, then gestured for Tilly to help her sit up in the bed.

Then she shot a vicious glare in Jamir's direction. "What is he doing in my fuckin' room?"

Everybody turned their gazes on Jamir.

"Because that is your brother, love" said LaVetra.

"That muthafucka ain't my brotha," said Heaven sharply, half of her head still wrapped up in a bandage in need of a dressing change.

"Hev," her mother stepped in.

"Get out." Heaven glared at Jamir, tempting the thought of spitting in his face. "Out," she screamed at him and winced from her own agony.

"Just give him a chance," said Monica.

"No." she shook her head. I don't want him near me at all. He's part of the reason I got a damn bullet in my fuckin head!"

Without a word Jamir headed for the door. LaShonda stared after her son and knew exactly what he was feeling at that moment. Then she turned a sharp gaze on Heaven and said, "You have no idea what we have been through behind all this goddamn foolishness, and you still, even after almost losing your damn life, can't sit your ass down for one minute to rationalize the situation."

That was when Monica moved next to LaShonda and rested a hand on her shoulder. Then she told her daughter the truth about everything.

There was no second-guessing the claims that her mother was laying on her. To hear that Jamir was her biological brother made her heart swell. But that was just the tip of the iceberg. Heaven was told of all the things that transpired while she was in her coma. The whole team had turned completely upside down in her absence and all she could do was shake her head sadly.

Finally, she broke down and cried, and all Monica could do was pull her daughter into her arms. They cried together, knowing how deep their troubles had become.

When her daughter arrived, it was the moment Heaven smiled and knew everything was gonna be alright. Then Anya and her son, Heaven's baby brother, Malik, arrived next and that was all it took to bring peace into her cold world.

"Is all forgiven, my love?" came LaVetra's words, after they all had settled down.

Heaven looked up at the elder woman.

"You have the power to control whatever it is that's been created behind my beloved nephew and his foolishness, Hev," she added.

"How can I forgive them, auntie?"

"I forgave Dejah," she said. "And your father was like a son to me, more than anythang. Your heart is too good to not forgive those who trespassed against you." LaVetra laid a gentle hand upon Heaven's leg as she stood at her bedside.

"You forgave Dejah?"

LaVetra smiled. "I sure did."

"And what did she say to that?"

"That she loves me and that she'll never do anything to break my heart again."

Even through the forgiveness in her brain after consuming all that she'd learned so far, Heaven could still visualize how that exchange between Dejah and LaVetra took place.

Forgiving those who once crossed her had always been hard for Heaven. So many people have died in the process of her decision to strikeout at her Hooliganz Crime Gang crew. The death of Veronica had hit her hard. She could just imagine what Thump and his mother were going through.

The door opened and Monique stumbled inside the room breathlessly, as though she had run all the way to the hospital. Heaven opened her arms to her girl and, once again, found herself crying upon the shoulder of someone else she loved.

After a while, Heaven looked out at those present amongst her and knew if it wasn't for them, she would have been dead a long time ago.

"Somebody go bring my brother back in here," Heaven requested, and Monica ran for the door to do just that.

"Jamir?" said Monique.

Heaven nodded.

"What're you about to do, Hev?" Monique looked at her suspiciously, remembering the last time Heaven had sent for Jamir. Things were so heated at that time, five people had died already.

"I must forgive him," said Heaven. Regardless what we been through together, I need to exercise forgiveness."

"This I must see then," said Monique.

"Then don't blink, bitch."

LaVetra smirked.

It was the start to a major evolution.

Chapter 7

Taquan was pacing back and forth, like a caged tiger. He had heard all about the hit at Da'Jhana's house and now she was nowhere to be found. He had called her phone a dozen times already, to no avail. His messages received no responses, as well. It was as if she was purposefully avoiding him, and that shit angered Taquan to the core.

After speaking with Naomi and Quesha about what they had witnessed Da'Jhana do, Taquan was scared for his girl. There was no telling what she was going through, at that moment. Could Da'Jhana be out there hunting for Duke, just as Taquan knew his team was? Both the Jr. Holliganz and the rest of the crew were out there looking everywhere for him, too.

Duke was a wanted man.

Another hooligan had to die.

While Mane pumped gas into his brother BowLegs' old Chevy Caprice Classic, he watched Taquan, yet again, try Da'Jhana's number for the thirteenth time. They were standing outside the Golden Falcon gas station off Martin L. King Blvd. after leaving the scene near Da'Jhana's house.

Also present was Skinny, Lil Eddie, and Marco, who was the oldest of the crew, having just pulled up on the scene after spotting the others,

"Where could that nigga be, though?" said Lil Eddie as he and Skinny exited the station.

"Put yourself in Duke's shoes for a minute. Knowing what he's faced wit' after what he did, where would he go, if not home? Who would he run to, besides us and Souljah, now that he's dead?" Taquan spoke up as they all gathered around the Chevy.

Skinny looked at Lil Eddie for an answer, but he didn't have one.

"Bully Gang," said Marco.

"Bingo," said Taquan with the snap of his fingers in exclamation of his point.

"Hell naw," Lil Eddie replied in disbelief. "Of all the muthafuckaz he could choose from—"

"Bully Gang will provide him protection that he needs in honor of his dead cousin. The blood on his hands killin' Tiwanna would seal the deal. Now it's time to make that move."

"We need to get at Jamir first, though," said Skinny, always down by protocol.

Taquan frowned at that but knew Skinny was right. Though he knew Jamir was busy taking care of the situation concerning Heaven, he would stop what he was doing to hear them out.

Jamir was still at the hospital. The crew headed there to consult with him before they made their next move.

"Lemme make a phone call first to see whether that's the deal or not," said Jamir.

"I'm tellin' you that's what he did," Taquan said. They were huddled up down the hall from Heaven's room. "Where else would he go?"

Jamir stood firm on what he said and separated himself from the circle to go make the call to Tito Sanders, who was one of Bully Gang's board members on count.

"This nigga's on some political shit," huffed Taquan.

"Mob shit."

"I'm on go-mode!"

Nobody responded to Taquan's obvious ranting. He was worried about Da'Jhana, and the more she remained unreachable, the darker his mind got.

Meanwhile, Kweli and Baiyina approached the crew, carrying mischievous looks on their faces. It was Bred man who had called them on it.

"She's plottin' on how to break Toby outta this place," said Kweli.

"And you're down wit' it too," said Taquan

Kweli didn't even deny it nor agree.

"Them people guardin' her ass back there, like she the President or somethin'. But shit, man, I'm down wit' it if y'all are," said LeLe, having just walked up on the conversation.

It was decided that HCG and Royal Mafia were now a team, after Heaven and Jamir gave the order to merge forces. It was no different from when HCG and Killa Don and his crew became allies. The thing with this union was that both empires were created from an official hooligan.

"I think I can help you accomplish that task," said another voice.

When all the heads swiveled in its direction, there stood Debra Moretti, the Italian mob queen and her loyal henchman. The crew had forgotten all about the female don until that very moment.

"And how's that?" asked Mane.

Right then, Jamir rejoined the circle. He then nodded at Debra respectfully before acknowledging his own crew.

"It's confirmed that Duke is now a Bully Gang affiliate," he said.

"I told you," Taquan sneered darkly.

"So, what's the next move?"

That's when Jamir turned his gaze directly on Taquan.

"I'ma give you that call to make, brah. However you choose to do it, I will support your decision fully," he exclaimed.

Taquan then let out that devilish grin of his. That was music to his ears.

"Okay," said Debra Moretti. "While you guys are focusing on that, I'll be seeing to Heaven's situation and what I can do for Toby." Then she and her four Italian goons turned and left them all staring after her.

"Am I trippin' or do that old Italian bitch got a whole lotta ass in that skirt she rockin'?" asked Mane with a funny face.

"You trippin'," said LeLe.

"I don't know, brah. She do look like she got something to sit on back there," said Skinny.

"And I thought you clowns had murder on your minds," Jamir shook his head and distanced himself away from them.

"So, what's up?" Bred Man spoke up.

"We wait til nightfall," said Taquan, "and then we gon press play on Bully Gang."

"Once again," added Baiyina.

"Once again."

Chapter 8

After driving around for a little while, White Boy Ty decided to take Shamoorah and his daughter out to the country to meet his uncle Bart. For the past hour or so, that was where they had been, while the rest of the world dealt with their own problems. He and Shamoorah had a lot of catching up to do. They had to fully reach a mutual understanding before taking it to another level.

"I'm not here to try to take Toby's place, Ty," said Shamoorah. "Destiny brough me here so that you could share a life with your daughter."

At that moment, Nikita was inside the house, asleep in Ty's old bedroom, while Abigail watched over her. Abigail was a loyal friend to Shamoorah, and had her best interest at heart. Sitting out on the steps of the back porch, smoking a blunt of Runtz weed, Ty looked up at Shamoorah standing before him with a piece of rabbit grass between her fingers.

"I want a life wit' her too," he said.

"But?"

"I don't wanna disappoint Toby."

She tossed the piece of grass down and turned away from him. Shamoorah looked out towards the four dog kennels enclosed inside a dome-like gate. Four pairs of eyes from the massively built Pitbull's stared back in her direction. Beyond the fenced in kennels was a large, wooded area that led to God-only-knows where.

"I wouldn't want you to disappoint her, Ty. She's also pregnant wit' your child. And I know you'll be a great, selfless father to those you have. I will not get in the way of your happiness."

Ty replied, "You once made me happy, too."

She turned to look at him. "Likewise."

"But?"

"Like I said before, Ty, I was young and too dumb to recognize the true good that's in you. I never gave you a chance because I was already taking a chance trusting you, a total stranger."

"A total stranger, huh?"

Shamoorah rolled her eyes at him. "Alright, I deserve everythang you throw at me right now. But rest assured, I will eventually earn your respect."

"Oh yeah?"

"Yep."

No sooner than the words left her mouth did three Royals suddenly step from around the corner of the house. When White Boy Ty saw this, he instantly shot to his feet and regarded them with open intrigue.

"What's going on, hooligan?"

"You see it," he said. "I'm chillin like a villain back here in the cut."

"Oh, we see," said Tilly, accompanied by Toosie and the vicious one, Hannah, who was a big two hundred ten pound solid bitch with light brown eyes.

"So, this is the one who thought shit was sweet to just come onto our territory and not get taxed?" replied Toosie, circling around Shamoorah.

"Ty, what's this shit? Who are these women?" asked Shamoorah as she shifted on her feet cautiously.

"Ty can't help you, boo." Tilly said.

Shamoorah gave him another questioning glance. When he just shrugged his shoulders, she already knew what she had to do from that point on.

"That ass gotta get taxed, if you think you gon' just—"

Without allowing Toosie to finish her statement, a fast and vicious left jab to the mouth, from Shamoorah, shut her up. The impact from the blow staggered Toosie. But Shamoorah was already rushing Hannah next, delivering two left-right hooks to her face.

"Ohh shit now," Tilly said as she watched Shamoorah battle it out with the two Royals. She looked over at Ty and caught a smirk on his face.

But of course, Shamorrah's fearlessness was noted, despite the beating she was taking now with Toosie and Hannah on her ass. It wasn't no easy feat because bowing down was not Shamoorah's intent, when the odds were against her. Shamoorah went pound for pound with them both, and never once hit the ground.

That was until Abigail came out of nowhere and started wearing Hannah's ass out with a thick wooden baseball bat she had apparently taken from Ty's old bedroom. That was all the advantage that was needed for Shamoorah to really get it in. Tilly wasn't having that. She drew her .44 Magnum and sent a shot into the sky. The blast from the cannon ceased all actions.

"Y'all back the fuck up. It's over," said Tilly. Then she looked over at White Boy Ty for a long moment before speaking. "She's official."

Ty nodded. "I already know."

"But what I wanna know, brah, is where does Toby stand, now that she's here?"

"Where she's been from day one, Tilly," he answered grudgingly. "And Shamoorah already know my heart is wherever Toby is."

"That's your word?"

"What you're gonna do, Tilly, is stop questioning my muthafuckin' loyalty to my bitch," he hissed at her.

Tilly threw her hands up in surrender. "A'ight then, brah. It's all love right here. I just really wanted to make sure Toby's heart was safe."

Tootsie spat out a glob of blood from her busted mouth and stuck our her hand to Shamoorah. Reluctantly, Shamoorah took her offered hand, and their respect was solidified. Hannah bumped fists with her, but then she glared in Abigail's direction. Abigail didn't even budge as she clutched the baseball bat in her hand.

"We good?" Tilly turned to Shamoorah and asked.

When she nodded in answer, Shamoorah turned away from her and walked back into the house through the open backdoor, where Uncle Bart stood.

In passing, Uncle Bart reached up to squeeze her shoulder affectionately and told Shamoorah that she was downright feisty.

"You heard about what Hev is demanding right now from her hospital bed, right?" asked Tilly.

"To rescue Toby?"

"That might already be in the making, but no," Tilly replied as she took a seat on the porch step next to Ty's standing position.

"Then what is it?"

"Rikah," said Tilly. "She's demanding to have Rikah brought back here to her."

That was when White Boy Ty knew that Heaven was back at it again. The bullet hole in her head wasn't even closed all the way up yet, and here she was still seeking vengeance.

"And what do you say?" he replied.

"I say we make it happen, but you already know how that's gonna turn out?"

"Rikah would have to die first."

Tilly nodded. "Because she damn sure ain't coming willingly when she knows her life would be over."

"It is what it is," White Boy Ty replied.

"It definitely is."

Chapter 9

A dignified dark-haired nurse in a well-fitting scrubs uniform with a flowered pattern came into the hospital room and checked one of the monitors tethered to Toby. Then the nurse nodded, tapped an IV line, nodded again and gave Toby a reassuring smile.

"Is there anything you need?" asked the nurse.

"I need everythang," Toby said. "But mainly, I need to get away from here."

"In due time, I'm sure you will."

Toby turned away from the other woman and didn't say anything further. She saw the look of pity in her eyes with her one good eye. She hated being pitied. People had been pitying her all her life, and she was sick of it. Toby had suffered multiple stab wounds from the prison-made shank, including the loss of one of her eyes, which was not bandaged over. For the remainder of her life, she would only have use of one eye.

But neither of those things mattered to her more than the life that was growing inside of her. Earlier on, the doctor had misjudged or misunderstood the procedure that took place regarding her unborn child, which was still in fetus embryo form. Where the doctor had declared the loss of her child, it was actually still very much alive and developing.

Through the storm and being beaten down, where many didn't survive, Toby and her unborn child survived. That was how Toby knew she had a true purpose in life, to create another life that would one day become something great in this world. And Ty would be there every step of the way, no matter the circumstances, he was right for it.

While Toby was swept into her troubled thoughts, she didn't right away perceive what the dark-haired nurse had slipped beneath her bed covering, until she finally spoke up.

"Courtesy of your brother, Delani. Just be careful with it, Toby," said the nurse.

Toby gazed up at her in obvious suspicion, then she felt around beneath the bed covering that she was lying beneath. When her fingers touched what she knew to be a cell phone, Toby felt her heart quicken with unsound excitement.

"You make sure you tell Delani it's a touchdown."

"What's your name?" asked Toby

The nurse grinned devilishly. "I'm Ranaja Brown," she said, and leaned in towards her ear to whisper something to her that made Toby smirk.

"I knew you looked familiar," said Toby.

"And you're still beautiful as ever, too." Nurse Brown patted her arm and turned for the door.

"Ranaja?"

She stopped, glanced back over her shoulder.

"Thank you."

With a nod, Nurse Brown opened the door and let herself out of the room.

Stroking the smooth exterior of the phone beneath her covers, Toby consumed herself in deep thought again. She had to play her position smartly now. Due to her predicament, she was being heavily guarded by government officials. There were three of them standing outside her room door right now. Normally, there would be one keeping her company inside, while the other two remained outside, guarding the premises. She would have to concoct a master plan to connect with her people, since neither her HCG crew nor her family members could visit with her. With that being said, she was going to have to be patient and wait on the universe to provide time for her. Communication was the key to surviving this situation, and she had all the communication that she needed right there in the bed with her.

Her first call would be to White Boy Ty, her king, her rock. Then she would hit Delani next, and together they would figure out how to win this game. Again, just when she was deep in thought, the door opened. This time it was Detective Angie Galloway who entered the room.

At the sight of the other woman, Toby watched as she approached her bedside and just stared down at her for a long moment before speaking.

"How you feelin', Toby?" asked Detective Galloway.

"Like brand new money," said Toby.

The detective smirked. "You always found strength and a sense of dignity in the face of conflict."

"Where is conflict?"

"Look at yourself right now, Toby. The life you chose to live is a conflict of its own. Yet, you've survived through the worst of them with your head high. But I'm not going to preach to you or upset you more than you already are," said the detective.

"Then why are you here, Angie?"

"First, to say thank you for what you did for my cousin, Kiara. That was very honorable of you, and I respect you for that."

"And?"

"And as you may already know, the person who attacked you is dead now. One of your girls saw to it that the matter was taken care of accordingly."

"Was she charged for it?"

Angie shook her head. "Due to the video surveillance in the pod, it showed her coming to your defense. The killin' was indeed justifiable and that's the way it is. So once again, despite your predicament, Toby, fate always seems to see things in your favor," she replied.

The reply Toby was tempted to deliver back to her, she knew the detective wouldn't find it favorably, so she decided to just keep her mouth shut.

"You saw Uncle Pete lately?" asked Toby.

"Yep."

"How is he?"

"He's still Petey," said the detective. "But since you asked, allow me to say he's been giving them people hell out there in concerns of your situation. And wanna know what's so amazing about it, too?"

"What?"

"He was sober," she said. "I think that's the first time in a long time I've seen Petey not high or drunk. But then again, maybe it's for the better."

"Maybe."

But little did they know, that was all Ty's doing. White Boy Ty knew the endless battles Toby and her uncle had to go through in regards of his addiction. Uncle Pete had once upon a time been a valuable asset to her and Delani's grind, at the beginning of their teaming up. Then, once she had gotten her weight up, Toby saw to the task of trying to clean her Uncle Pete up in the process. But the man was too stubborn, it only created more problems between her and him.

Then Ty came along and became more persistent in seeing that Uncle Pete at least sobered up for a change. It was a challenging feat, but it turned out that Uncle Pete had finally given himself a chance. Toby was proud of him. It almost made her cry to hear that.

Chapter 10

After spending a few hours with Heaven to assure her that she would always be there to support her, Monique finally took her leave. She was emotionally exhausted. It was hard enough having to watch Heaven wither away for multiple weeks, while in a coma, only to awaken to the truths of her own terrifying creation.

One of those truths was the deaths of Veronica and her loved ones. Their childhood friend-sister, the one who pretty much was the link to their sisterhood. Monique wondered how Heaven would feel to learn that her visit today wasn't solely about supporting her. She was on a mission, too, and that mission was to find out who was the actual murderer of her dear friend. She had to come seeking for answers.

When she exited the hospital, a car was already waiting for her out front. It was a black-on-black Mercury with dark tinted windows. Monique opened the door and got into the front passenger seat.

"How lil sis doing?" Thump asked from behind the wheel as he drove away from the hospital's entrance.

Monique replied, "Hev is doing okay. Her wounds are healing progressively and the doctor said she would have a speedy recovery, now that she's up. She will begin physical therapy in a few days."

He nodded.

"She asked about you, and mama, too."

"What you told her?" asked Thump. Since returning from out of town, all Thump was focused on was being supportive to his mama. He was grieving hard over the loss of Veronica and his loved ones. Thump was just playing his cards close and staying in the shadows until he got his man. He didn't want to go against Royal Mafia and HCG, he wouldn't be able to beat those odds, he wasn't that stupid.

Thump was always a solo act. He did all his dirt all by his lonesome.

Finding his sister's killer was top priority now. He wasn't gonna target the whole team and risk the chance of dying in the process, before he avenged Veronica's death. Plus, he knew the Feds were watching now, too. He'd spotted a few undercover agents in the field, lurking and trying to blend in.

Can't be too careful, he thought.

It happened the evening he got back in town from off the road. He went straight to his mama's house, which had become a crime scene. That's when he noticed that he was being followed. While he was being watched, he watched out for those who were watching him, which meant that he needed to move with caution and not step out of course and get himself cased up.

Thump would play this mission out as quietly and thoroughly as possible. He just wanted the person responsible.

"I only told her what she already expected to know," said Monique.

"You didn't mention nothin' about the mission?"

"Now why would I do that?" Monique shot him a look of contempt for even insinuating such a thing. "But on the other hand, I feel like I'm betraying Hev somehow. Thump, I mean, I want the person who killed Veronica to pay for what they did. But it's hard to also look Hev in the eyes, knowing I'm helping you on the low to find someone that she prolly also care about, too."

"So, you don't think she wants to find out who killed Vee and punish them for it?" he asked.

Monique shrugged her shoulder.

"Answer me, Mo!"

"I don't know, brah. It ain't like we had the time to actually talk about it, wit' everybody around vying for her attention."

"You were in that bitch for damn near three hours!"

She stiffened. "We didn't talk about it."

"Don't worry about it," Thump mumbled to himself. "I'll see to it that it gets done once and for all. And if Heaven gets in my fuckin' way, then she's gonna get the same issue as the muthafucka who took my sista away from me."

You could literally hear the venom in his words when he spoke.

"I'm gonna drop you off back at the house, lil sis."

"What're you finna do, Thump?" Monique had a bad feeling he was about to do something crazy.

Before he could answer, the car stopped two cars back from a red-light intersection downtown on the corner next to the old historical courthouse on Pat Thomas Highway. A second later, the driver's window exploded from a deafening blast from the pump-action shotgun that came into view. Monique screamed bloody murder when the side of her face was sprayed with Thump's blood and pieces of flesh.

The impact from the gun had blown Thump's left shoulder into a bloody mess. Then the driver's door opened as a hand reached in to drag Thump out of the car.

"No. Stop," Monique screamed again when she saw the big gun aimed down at Thump's head before it exploded again.

Boom!

Chapter 11

When it really came down to catching a muthafucker lacking, when they least expected it, nighttime was the best time to execute a plan of attack. Most people would be so tired from steady being busy throughout the day that once night fell, their bodies began to unwind. They became laxed and comfortable, and mentally unstable in a sense.

The night could be very dangerous for some people. It was a time where the wickedest things happened and no one would be the wiser.

The demons came out at night. And so did the hooliganz, as Booby, LJ, Delani, Mookie, Bizzy and Shoo Baby entered Yonkers territory, like a pack of wolves on the trail of a wounded beast. But they weren't the only ones prowling through the night, for Yonkers, too, had it's share of hooligans, Killaz and hoodlums alike. Though to Holliganz Crime Gang, all of them muthafuckers were collateral damage, if they made it their business to intervene.

This was more the reason to play their hands smart, so as not to create additional problems than what they were already faced with, where the life of death of Damian was of concern.

So tonight, both Shoo Baby and Mookie would initiate the mission. Two beautiful women were more trustful to let your guard down and welcome into your home than two niggas.

The house in question was located on Elm Street. Theo Graham and his wife, Nikki, lived there with their two biological children, Theo Jr. and Camillah, and their adopted god daughter, Chloe. Both parents were elementary school teachers, one math and the other art. And they had no clue the tragedy they were about to experience.

"Y'all ready?" asked LJ from the leading car as it approached the house up the street from where Delani and his team were occupying another car, just seven houses down.

Shoo Baby lifted the walkie-talkie communicator to her mouth to respond.

"Just sit back and watch me work, my nigga," Shoo Baby firmly responded.

LJ chuckled and glanced over at Bizzy in the front passenger seat next to him. "That damn Shoo Baby is the real deal."

In the car up ahead were both women hooliganz, along with Booby behind the wheel. Although he was deaf, Booby was a damn good driver, when you needed one. The nigga was official behind the wheel. The car stopped outside of the Graham's house, and without hesitation, both Shoo Baby and Mookie got out and made their way to the front door.

The driveway, where Delani and his crew got inside their car, belonged to an associate of Diva, whom she persuaded to share an evening supper with at a local upscale diner, while the hooliganz took care of their business. At the door was Shoo Baby, who used her charm to gain entrance into the house. After Mookie had followed her inside, it wasn't even three minutes later when their communicator confirmed their position.

"Everythang is secured," acknowledged Mookie, while her partner-in-crime went about finding something to bound them.

"Ten-Four," LJ responded.

"A'ight. Y'all know your roles and position," Delani said to the other two. "T'night we serve this nigga that gangsta and then we gone."

"Say no more," LJ nodded.

"Let's go," Delani told Bizzy, and they got out the car and took the sidewalk towards the house.

A minute later, Delani walked through the door into the house. Bizzy took his position in the shadows alongside the house, out of sight.

"They got a door-cam surveillance," said Mookie. "I peeped it before we cane in the spot. I'm about to dismantle that bitch and dispose of it."

"Good lookin', my nigga. Go do your thang." Delani then stood by and watched Mookie threaten the well-being of the children if either of the parents didn't tell her what she needed to know.

Meanwhile, Shoo Baby ran the game down to the wife and what she needed to do to get Damian there to the house, without alarming him.

"I knew it," cried Nikki Graham. "I knew one day he would bring trouble to our font door." The tears spilled from her eyes in big droplets.

"It's simple, if you'd just calm down," said Mookie.

"I'll do it," said Theo. He was a tall, lanky guy with deep dimples in his cheeks. "I won't disappoint you, just as long as you don't hurt our children."

"The kids are safe," said Delani. "All we want is Damian, and we'll leave you alone."

"And you expect for me to believe that you'll just leave us be after you do God-knows-what to him? I'm not green, young man. You're gonna kill us afterward. There's a reason you're not disguising your identities from us. It's because the endgame is to leave no stone unturned, no witnesses."

"Theo?"

"Just shut the hell up!"

Nikki frowned, her face still wet from her tears. Then she looked up at Delani and said to him, "Make the call."

He was happy to oblige.

They made the call.

Chapter 12

Back home in Quincy, the Jr. Hooliganz were on the move and hungry for some traitor's blood. In the process, Duke was still nowhere to be found, but alive and well, despite the circumstances. It was wild how he'd been locked up all that time, only to come home and become marked for death on the same damn day. He had yet to go home and spend some quality time with his mother. He only saw her once, earlier that day at the black party, before Taquan made the stress call.

But Da'Jhana, who'd been lurking outside of Duke's mother's house all evening, was praying and hoping he'd throw caution to the wind and bring his ass home. All she needed was an opportunity to bust his fuckin' head.

Since leaving the murder scene at her house earlier, Da'Jhana had been searching high and low for Duke. It was as though he'd vanished off the face of the earth. Inside the house, Duke's mother, Val, was running herself crazy, calling everybody in search of her eldest child. There were three more siblings, two girls and a boy, all of whom Duke had advised to join HCG for the opportunity to get money and help his mother provide for their household.

Three times now Val had left the house to go look for Duke and not found him. She had just gotten back five minutes ago, slouching back into the house, exhausted from her ordeal. Duke was not coming home tonight.

He knew it was a trap, knew that if he stood a chance of surviving this, he had to skip town and never come back.

But the tables turned when suddenly Da'Jhana heard Val's phone ring beyond the window of her own bedroom.

"Duke," his mother cried out.

Da'Jhana became stoic as she brought her head closer to the bedroom window to listen more clearly.

Inside the room, through the worn, thin curtains, Val had been sitting on the foot of her bed, rolling up a nice joint of weed. Then the phone rang and she all but dived across the bed to retrieve it form the nightstand. Now she was standing up with her back toward the bedroom window.

"Where the hell are you, baby? You got us worried sick over you," said Val.

This was Da'Jhana's shot for vengeance.

"In Midway? Wit' who? Never mind that, when are you coming home? Your sistaz and baby brotha is crying for you. They heard 'bout what happened to your cousin earlier. What's going on, Duke, cause I can't take no more of this shit? I need you home wit' us." Val sounded on the verge of hysterically losing grip of herself.

Almost like Da"Jhana when she saw her dead sister, but that emotion had changed to pure hate, and now all she cared about was payback. The fear in Val's voice was clear. She knew her first born was in a world of trouble. From what she gathered from the rest of the one-sided conversation between Duke and his mother, he wanted her to bring him some things from his room that he had put away. Then Val was given the location where she agreed to meet with Duke to deliver the items that he stressed he was in dire need of.

"I'm on my way right now, sugar." Duke's mother told him, after he told her he loved her.

With that being said, Da'Jhana took off running through the night, up the street and around the corner, where she left Tiwanna's car parked next to a Baptist church. She would then follow Duke's mother to where she planned to meet him. There Da'Jhana would finally get her wish to end his life, And her misery.

She didn't ask for this life, it was forced upon her, and now she must play her part.

Upon reaching the car Da'Jhana opened the door and got in behind the wheel. Then instinct kicked in and she reached for her gun, at the same time, a hand gripped her wrist in the darkness.

"It's just me, Daj. It's me."

She paused. "Taquan?"

He released her and told Da'Jhana to shut the door. Reluctantly, she did as he asked of her and Taquan removed the fitted cap he was wearing.

"I've been lookin' all over for you, Daj," he said softly. "But then again, I figured you was out there lookin' for that nigga who killed your sista."

"And I found him, too," she said.

Taquan was taken aback by her statement. "You found him? Where?" he demanded. He didn't tell her that he also had BredMan watching Duke's mother's house as well. BredMan had even reported back to him that he had spotted Da'Jhana also lurking in the shadows.

With a tone of sharp intensity, Da'Jhana told him what she had just learned back at the house. In doing so, a pair of headlights illuminated the night as a white Toyota turned on the street at their left.

"Speakin' of the devil," muttered Taquan. He had mad love for Duke's mother, she was cool as a fan, and it bothered him that he had to break her heart.

Da'Jhana proceeded to follow the white Toyota, while not trying to get too close to be detected.

"Midway," said Taquan.

"That's what she said," she replied.

In turn, Taquan told her about his meeting with Jamir earlier.

"So, he done switched over on the enemy's side now?"

"His loyalty was to his cousin, which was all the right for Bully Gang to accept him, especially after he did what he did." Then before he could talk himself out of it, Taquan leaned over to place a gentle kiss upon her cheek. "We gon' get that nigga, Daj."

Taking out his phone, Taquan sent his crew a text message to discreetly inform them about the new development.

"I also had my mama to go ahead and make funeral arrangements for big sis. She said that she would get wit' Uncle Rodney to make the necessary contacts to get it situated."

"You didn't have to do that, Quan."

"Somebody had to do it," said Taquan firmly. "She was like a sista to me, too, you know."

"I know," she sighed.

He reached over and cranked up the sound system a little bit to fill the void of intense silence between them. Moments later, sounds of Boston Richey were seeping from the speakers as they followed the White Toyota to its next destination.

Chapter 13

Finally, night had fallen and he could move around like he wanted to, without worrying about being seen by potential threats. A slight chance of rain was predicted. Damian was sitting in a dark, unmarked Ford pickup, parked on the side street, roughly five hundred yards down the road from Theo Graham's place.

When he got the call from Nikki, saying there was a family emergency back home in Newark, New Jersey, where her presence was needed, and asking if he could watch his daughter for them for a few days, that gave Damian pause. Of all the people she could have asked and would be granted immediately, she chose him. Damian didn't believe it had something do with him being locked up and not being able to spend time with his daughter, like he should. He smelled something fishy about the whole situation. He already had trust issues.

Plus, he knew Nikki Graham didn't like him very much. She was Damian's dead baby mama, Stephanie Miller's best friend since high school and had always thought he wasn't good for her friend. Nikki never trusted him.

Now, here she was trusting him with Chloe?

Bullshit, Damian had thought. But he had stopped what he was doing to make the drive out to Yonkers.

Before the call came, Damian was scheming on this young Harlem dude, who was said to be getting to the bag. His name was Trap Boi Winslow, another ex-con, who got out of prison and was using his street profits to invest in lucrative businesses. Damian wanted a piece of that pie and was building a plan to get it.

The wolves out there gotta eat, too.

But this bullshit with Nikki summoning him over to the house may postpone that feast. The whole way over, Daimian had convinced himself something else was up.

It just didn't feel right.

Damian had always listened to his first mind, and it spared him many failures in life, which is why he decided to park nearby and watch before he made his move. Being cautious and observant always paid off in due time.

After thirteen minutes of watching, his patience indeed paid off with the strike of a lighter inside a car parked in the driveway of a house nearby. This whole time someone had been occupying the car, in the dark of night, waiting for something or someone in particular?

A murderous sneer appeared on Damian's face as he now zeroed in on the car in the driveway, the threat. Danger, Damian sensed he was waiting on him.

Being that as it may, could Nikki have played a part in setting him up for the kill? Could his daughter be in grave danger right now?

Without second guessing the matter, Damian armed himself and slipped from the truck quietly. He was already at work lurking tonight, so his all-back attire blended in well with the shadowy night. He was armed with his fully loaded .45-caliber Remington 1911 pistol and his 12-inch Huntsman Blade with the natural bone handle. In this situation, he preferred to initiate brutal force with his knife, so as not to alert any other potential threats who were probably waiting for him inside the house.

Through the shadows of the night, he crept all the way over to the parked car in the driveway. He could smell the Black & Mild cigar smoke wafting from the car when he eased up to the driver's door from the blind side. The nigga inside didn't even have a clue he was a dead man.

Moving with stealth and precision, Damian snatched the door open, and for a fleeting moment, he recognized the nigga's face when the dome light came on. It was the very same nigga he remembered seeing earlier that day going into the law office building, the very same law firm where Nancy worked. And the very same bitch who knew about Chloe and where she lived. *Nancy set me up?* He wondered to himself. Damian had determined this fact in the fraction of an instant, upon seeing LJ's face and putting the pieces together.

"You bitch ass nigga," Damian snarled, and swiped the blade across LJ's throat, just as he reached for the gun sitting in his lap. The he lunged forward and stabbed LJ in the chest area multiple times, killing him right the behind the wheel of the car. Then he turned his wicked gaze toward the house, where he knew more trouble awaited.

LJ didn't stand a chance.

Neither did the others.

Chapter 14

From where he stood, hidden in the shadows along the house, Bizzy had witnessed the whole thing. He knew LJ was dead. The killing had been swift and quiet, compared to certain murders he was used to. Bizzy was sure the killer was Damian, and the way it went down just now made him a little nervous.

From the distance, Bizzy watched as the dark clothed killer disappeared between the space of the row of houses along his side of Elm Street. Bizzy though like a killer, as he was one by trade. He knew from the way things looked, Damian would be taking the back way to reach the house unnoticed.

Bizzy already had his gun ready to announce his presence just as soon as Damian showed up. Pressing his back against the wall of the house and squatting down low in position, Bizzy watched intensively and listened carefully. Would Damian actually walk into his demise right now? He wondered. Would he make his own death that easy, as LJ's had been, just moments ago?

No more than a couple minutes later, Bizzy detected movement on his right. Sure enough, it was Damian, having finally crept his way through the dark to reach the house.

Damian hurried across to the back of the Graham's house and Bizzy waited for his moment. Knowing what type of caliber Damian was, and having him so close to him after watching him murder another hooligan, made Bizzy kind of intimated for a moment. The nigga was totally oblivious to the threat that now rose up to take his shot.

In the movies, the killer always had some slick-talk witty bullshit to say before he executed his man. But this moment was reality, Bizzy had no parting words for Damian. He aimed his .9mm Rugar and squeezed the trigger. Rushing forward, he gunned his man down right where he stood.

Damian cried out and hit the ground hard. Seeing this, Bizzy walked up to the fallen killer and stood over him. Damian had taken four slugs to his body and was still breathing.

"Tell the Devil Bizzy said he'll meet him one day," said Bizzy before he sent two more bullets slamming into Damian's face, killing him dead.

"It's a wrap," Bizzy spoke into the walkie-talkie communicator to those inside. "Damian is dead," he said.

Moments later, the front door opened and the hooliganz poured out into the night. When Bizzy showed them Damian's dead corpse, Delani nodded. Then Bizzy delivered the sad news about what happened to LJ.

Mookie gasped and ran for the car. LJ still sat slumped behind the wheel.

"Oh no," she cried.

"We can't leave him like that," said Delani angrily. He was hurt that LJ didn't make it out alive to see his own mission accomplished. Together they laid LJ into the backseat of the car and, with Shoo Baby behind the wheel now, they got the hell out of dodge.

"Fuck! Fuck! Fuck!" Delani slammed a fist into the palm of his gloved hand to emphasize his anger, having lost another of his own.

"This shit crazy," said Shoo Baby as she led the way out of Yonkers back where it was safe.

Behind them, Booby, Mookie and Bizzy were going through the same troubles over LJ's death.

"We cannot let anyone outside the crew, such as the cops, know about LJ. That's all it takes for them crackaz to link us and find out this where we at now," said Delani sadly. He also knew Heaven was really not going to like this at all. LJ would have to be permanently disposed of now.

It is what it is.

It ain't like he can complain about it.

Better to be safe than sorry.

Chapter 15

The Flying J's Truck Stop was where Val had eventually turned into the entrance of and parked outside the building's main service door.

About fifty yards back Da'Jhana and Taquan drove past with Taquan spinning around in his seat to keep an eye on Val's movements. She had gotten out of the car, with a duffle bag in her hand, and entered through the main entrance of the building with it.

A little ways up the street, Da'Jhana parked the car off to the side of the highway. She didn't want Duke to have the chance of recognizing Tiwanna's car and panicking and running away.

But the stolen Mazda that Bred Man, Von and Lil Eddie were riding in couldn't be identified. It turned into the entrance of the truck stop and circled around the large building once, before parking next to a service gas pump.

"We're in position, brah. I got eyes on the nigga as we speak," said Von into the phone.

"What about any company he might have wit' him?"

"He's solo, besides his old girl."

Taquan said, "Watch that muthafucka closely, Von."

"Gotcha," was the reply.

"Can I ask you a question, Quan?" Da'Jhana replied, having been quiet pretty much the whole ride over. Taquan turned to look at her, and she said, "Put yourself in Duke's shoes for a minute, would you have done the same thang?"

"You asking would I have told my cousin?"

She nodded her head.

Taquan didn't answer her right away, he had asked himself the same question several times already. "I am family oriented, Daj, you know that. But I think it depends on how close I am wit' them compared to where I stand wit' my team."

"So, 'blood is thicker than water' doesn't always apply to you?" she wanted to know.

"Family are mostly the ones who'll cross you before anybody else would?"

"Would you have done it, Quan?"

"No."

"Because you know what Hooliganz Crime Gang would do to you if you did," she said simply. Taquan didn't even have a response to that because it was true. HCG was by far the deadliest organization in the area and was steady growing by the number.

The text came that Duke was back on the move again, but this time he was doing the unexpected.

"He's in one of the rigs, brah," said Von excitedly. "The nigga is gettin' away in a fucking eighteen-wheeler."

"Which one?"

"The big red 18-wheeler with the orange and red neon fire flames going along the side of the rig." Why Duke was attempting to get away in one of the rigs driven by some accomplice was baffling.

"So he wasn't planning on staying wit' Bully Gang after all," exclaimed Da'Jhana as she watched the big rig ease its hulking frame towards the exit of the truck stop.

"That's what it looks like."

"So, what now?"

He was brooding over the matter for a moment.

By this time, the big 18-wheeler was pulling out into traffic, coming up behind the Infiniti along the highway, heading north towards Tallahassee.

"Hold up," muttered Taquan. He then reconnected with Vonte and inquired about Lil Eddie and the Mac-90 he knew his hooligan was carrying with him.

"What about it, brah?"

"Make the whole thang go boom," said Taquan. When he said that Da'Jhana looked over at him, wanting to ask what he meant by that.

"Say less," answered Von and disconnected.

A minute later, the big rig roared past the Infiniti as Da'Jhana waited to follow suit. She figured Von and his crew in the Mazda would want to tail the 18-wheeler closer to carry out the hit.

"It's almost over, baby," Taquan told her.

Da'Jhana didn't say anything.

After a while, the Infinite pulled onto the highway behind the team of hooliganz before them. In the darkness of the car, Taquan reached over and took her by the hand. He lifted it over toward his face and kissed the back of her hand. The quiet affection was not lost on her. Da'Jhana knew that he loved her, it was why they were even together right now. Lord knows she needed it because she didn't have nothing else, everything she ever wanted after losing her brother Broozy was gone.

Now Tiwanna was gone and it hurt.

"Everythang gone be all right," Taquan promised her, and she could only hope that it was true.

Seven minutes later, they watched as multiple .223 rounds from Lil Eddie's assault rifle penetrated the rig's large gas tank. The truck exploded and causing damn near everything its proximity to become subjected to destruction as well. The Infiniti drove right past the disaster.

Von and the others were safe.

And Duke was dead.

He damn well had to be.

Chapter 16

White Boy Ty was up before dawn, startled awake by a dream where a pistol-packing Toby speeding down South Jackson Street, blasting at him with his daughter Nikitta riding next to him in the passenger seat. Ty could even feel the slugs tearing into him in the dream.

He eased from the bed, letting Shamoorah sleep. She could barely sleep last night, still amped up with what happened between her and the Royals. After a nice hot shower, Ty went up front, where he found Abigail standing in the kitchen. She was bare feet in a pair of basketball shorts and a sports bra to show off her tight physique. Abigail was pretty, with a soft caramel skin tone, walnut brown eyes and far from shy.

Also, present was little Chloe, all eleven months old and sweet as pecan pie. She was sitting on the kitchen counter and Abigail was feeding her some of the scrambled eggs she had made. The aroma of freshly cooked breakfast permeated the kitchen, and apparently Chloe' was enjoying her share.

"There's scrambled eggs, toast and bacon on the stove if you want anything to eat."

"I see you've made yourself at home," he retorted.

"Any kitchen is my home, Ty."

"So, you cook?" He moved toward the stove.

Abigail shrugged and suddenly baby girl was no longer interested in food, she wanted her daddy. Chloe pretty much pushed Abigail away and opened out her arms to him.

White Boy Ty scooped her right up into his arms. The child beamed up at him. In a way, Ty believed the child already knew that he was her daddy. Shamoorah claimed that she never brought any men around Chloe for fear of her becoming attached. But just as soon as Ty first held her in his arms, Chloe somehow automatically knew that was where she truly belonged. And since then, what little time they had together already, they'd become almost inseparable. While Ty cuddled with his daughter, Abigail took it upon herself to fix his plate of food.

"Bart had his breakfast already," said Abigail. "He's gone out wit' his boat to the lake for some fishin' time." She sat his plate onto the kitchen table and poured him a fresh cup of cold milk.

"Thank you," Ty sat down in front of his plate of food with Chloe in his lap.

Abigail sat down across from him.

"So how did you two eventually meet up? Because what I was told was that she left all those she loved behind, back in Orlando?"

"She did," said a humbled Abigail.

Ty gestured for her to continue while he ate his food and shared with his daughter.

"I was already away from home by the time she ran away. I was living down in Miami, finishin' up my associates degree in radiology."

"Did it work out?" he asked.

She shook her head no.

"What happened?"

"Got caught up wit' this Miami clown and his thuggish charisma and money, and got too sidetracked to give a damn about finishin' up my final semester. That's when I bumped into Shamoorah."

"Oh shit," muttered White Boy Ty, thinking back on the day when he first bumped into Shamoorah.

"She was eight months pregnant then," she said. "Shamoorah is the reason I packed up and left that clown. We got us an apartment down in the Florida Keys area and was doing good up until she learned what was going on up here wit' y'all."

"Answer this question for me, Abigail."

"What?"

"Is her family really rich?"

The question seemed to affect Abigail in a way, and she let out a troubling breath before she spoke. "Yes. Her daddy is a major boating business owner, who sells small engine boats to super yachts for a living. Her mom is a retired airplane stewardess who spends her days pampering herself and mingling wit' the rich folks and politicians," said Abigail.

"But that's not the life Shamoorah wants."

"No."

All Ty could do is shake his head. Coming from where he came from, and all those he associated himself with in the process, he knew people who'd murder their own family to have a life like that.

"Shamoorah," Abigail persisted evenly. "She's different, Ty. One can grow to love and appreciate the person she is, not who her parents led her out to be."

"What about you?"

"Me?"

"Yeah. What's your life like?"

That's when she smiled. "II was the black sheep in my family before I lost them in a house fire when I was twenty."

"Damn. That's fucked up. So, what now?"

"I was hoping you can answer that question for me, now that I'm here." She looked him dead in the eyes.

"So, you tellin' me you're staying here now? What about your spot down in the Keys?"

"It was temporary anyway," she told him. "And besides, I kinda like this country town. Y'all get it in up here. I can appreciate a place like this."

"Be careful what you wish for," Ty replied.

Chapter 17

Three days later, Harold paced the floor of the jail's lobby, biting his bottom lip anxiously. When he received the call from his wife half an hour ago, he came running to the jailhouse. The courts saw it in her favor to release Kiara, now that they got Toby for the crime. Her bold testimony was the key to freeing Kiara, and she would be forever grateful to her for that.

Although Kiara tried to save Toby that night of the murder, Toby still managed to own up to her business in order to save Kiara.

Toby was content with her decision.

She was loyal.

Just when he was about to lose his patience, the side door next to the security station booth opened up. Kiara stepped through the door. Harold felt his heart skip a beat and then she rushed into his arms.

"Oh baby, I love you wit' all my heart."

"Get me away from here, Harold," she pleaded. Her husband nodded and then escorted her toward the exit.

Standing just outside the door, talking on his cellphone, was Preach. When he saw Kiara, he all but screamed and shouted with extreme joy. He hugged Kiara, kissed her on the cheek, and hurried off to get the car.

"Take me home," demanded Kiara, once she was finally inside the car.

"Say no more," Preach complied.

Leaning her head upon her husband's shoulder in the backseat, Kiara finally allowed herself to cry. Harold pulled her closer and just let her have her moment. There were no words needed to be said. Kiara cried all the way home. Harold helped her out of the car and into the house.

"I need a long bath for now," she said. Kiara then left the men standing in the living room, looking after her with mixed emotions.

Harold dropped down into his favorite chair and let out a long breath. "Thank you, Lord, for bringin' my baby back home to us," he prayed.

"God is good, brotha."

"He is merciful," Harold nodded. "Oh. This one here deserves a good strong one, huh, Preach?"

Preach was already up on his feet, heading into the kitchen to pour them both a glass of Crown Royal to celebrate Kiara's return.

Meanwhile, there was a knock on the front door. Harold got up to go answer it. To his surprise, it was Angie standing on his doorstep, and she wasn't alone because Linda Keaton from next door was standing right beside her. Linda, he was okay with, but Harold didn't feel too kindly about Angie being there. Without a word, he stood aside and allowed the two women to enter.

"I really need to see her," said Angie.

"Is something wrong?" Harold asked.

The detective shook her head no. She said, "I just wanna make sure she's okay."

"Me too," added Linda.

With a shrug, Harold said that Kiara was busy taking a bath at the moment. It was as if he didn't say a damn thing because the women still hurried through the house toward the back to be with Kiara anyway.

"Here you go, brotha." Preach walked up and handed Harold his drink. "Just how you like it."

Twenty minutes later, Angie took her leave, and five minutes after that, Linda saw herself out. Then Kiara emerged soon afterwards, looking refreshed and dressed in her usual casual wear and sandals. One look at her and Harold was proud to have had made her his wife.

"I want to go see Toby," she announced. Harold already had her favorite glass of wine before her. She accepted it humbly, but didn't drink from it right away. "It is very detrimental that I see her."

"That can't wait till tomorrow?"

"No," she said

"But you just got home, Kay," Harold argued. "Hell, if it wasn't for her you—"

"Don't even go there, Harold. Because if it wasn't for her, a whole lot of other thangs woulda gone wrong and we'd still be suffering from it right now." Kiara checked her husband and all Harold could do was respect her mind. After all, she was right. Toby's presence in their lives was meaningful, and her devotion to those she loved and cared about would never go unappreciated.

Bitches like her were a godsend.

Toby was a blessing.

So, to the hospital they went so Kiara could visit with Toby and ease her broken heart a little. Little did she know, they would find out once they got there that Toby was already gone. Yep. It was all so true.

The hooliganz had struck again.

Chapter 18

Since the vicious killings of Souljah, Duke and Thump, the HCG crew had been laying low and staying off the radar. When it was considered that Thump posed a serious threat over what went down with his family's murders, Erick and Lil One saw to it that he was dealt with accordingly. He was moving too quietly and suspiciously humble for a person who'd just lost several of his family members. Lil One literally obliterated Thump's face. The shit was gruesome.

And so was Duke's demise. His murder was still being viewed on the local news stations three days later. His mama, Val, was making a major scene about it. She was even screaming Bully Gang was to blame for the murder, which was music to the hooliganz' ears, little did mama know.

But the heat was on, and the cops were once again rounding niggas up, questioning them relentlessly about the recent murders. The day when Thump got killed, Monique was taken in for questioning. The hit transpired a half of block away from the Quincy Police Station. Right there in front of the downtown historical courthouse.

Monique kept it true and didn't speak a word against the hooliganz. Though the two homicide detectives interrogating her were intimidating and trying to get her to implicate HCG for the murder, Monique all but spat in their faces. They roughed her up a little, getting her out of there, and Monique took it with pride.

It was also believed that Thump was being followed by two FBI agents during the incident. When the hit was going down, their car was also stuck at an intersection and couldn't make it there in time to catch the shooter. They were still scratching their heads on that.

They were too slow on the draw down and now relied on intense investigative leads to get them their man. They relied on the traffic cam to get the job done, and not even that was supportive enough because Lil One was well-hidden in disguise behind a non-penetrable mask. They would have to go deep into their grid to come up with a hit.

And it won't be long either.

After a few days, Heaven sent for Monique, and she was found and retrieved within the hour. This was during the time when Harold was escorting his wife home from the county jail. Seventeen minutes later, Detective Galloway had left her hospital room to go check in on her cousin.

Heaven felt some type of way, after learning that Monique was in that car with Thump. Knowing his intentions were to seek harm against her team, she felt Monique had betrayed her trust by not telling her what was going on.

"You could've been killed, too," Heaven had told her, when her friend pleaded her case.

"So, what now? Are you gonna sit there and not do nothing about who killed Veronica, too?"

Heaven just looked at her.

"So, you're protectin' them," said Monique. "I get it. Your loyalty is to your team. Obviously, Veronica's life didn't mean nothing to you to begin wit'."

That's when Heaven hauled off and slapped her. Monique was startled and looked at her friend in astonishment. Then her eyes clouded over with unmistakable fury as she glared at Heaven.

"I loved Veronica," Heaven hissed at her. "She was my sista, too, Mo! Shit just got outta control and she was caught in the crossfire."

"You can't justify that shit." Monique clenched her fists.

Tilly and LadyBug moved in unison to separate Heaven and Monique, since she had that look in her eyes.

"Back the fuck up off her," Heaven looked at her two Royals and said, "I got this shit."

No sooner than the words left her mouth did the blare of the fire alarm sound off throughout the hospital. Then, all of a sudden, it was total chaos in the building.

Two more Royals, Anya, Zamon and Monica suddenly stormed through the door into the room moments afterward. By this time, Heaven was demanding to get out of bed. Monique and Tilly were assisting her with doing so.

"Is there really a fire?" asked Heaven curiously.

"I haven't noticed the likes of one," Monica answered as she reached for her cellphone. "I don't know what's going on in this place," she said.

Heaven was deposited into a wheelchair and was about to be wheeled over to the door before it opened. Two big burly-looking Italian gangsters entered the room and said they had come in care of Debra Moretti to see that Heaven was safely taken care of.

"I have my own people for that," said Heaven. "Thank you."

"We're just following orders, ma'am," said the shorter one, who was also wide as the door.

"I'll reassure her that your duty was fulfilled."

Both Italians nodded their thick heads graciously but made no move to leave the room.

"Are y'all gonna move the fuck out the way or do we have to make you?" Zamon asked impatiently, not caring about them being mob guys, for he would step on them just as he would any other.

"There's no fire in the building," said the short one. "It's just a diversion, among other things."

"A diversion?" Anya frowned.

"For what?" said Heaven.

"For Toby to get out of the building safely through the chaos," he said. "Our other guys are seeing to that task as we speak."

"So y'all are breakin' Toby out?" asked Tilly.

He nodded.

"By now, she should be gone already," he provided.

And Tilly couldn't help herself, she smiled. There was no doubt in her mind it was true.

Chapter 19

The escape was big news. The newspapers and TV news led with it for days. There was immediate speculation as to whether Royal Mafia or Hooliganz Crime Gang had had anything to do with the escape and whether the assumed bad blood between the two groups was still existent. But the assumption was short-lived when witnesses spotted both parties mingling with one another during a local fundraiser event in support of the children's hospital cancer patients. The building was in need of some serious repair. The two organizations teamed up four days after the escape to give back to the community.

As he sat poolside behind Dejah's mansion, reading the daily news report regarding the happenings down in Quincy, Shamar was not surprised to hear that Toby had escaped.

"I'm not even surprised it happened," said Dejah, lounging next to him, sipping champagne and smoking on something so potent it made Shamar's nostrils cringe.

"I wonder where she's been taken to. In her condition, she would need constant treatment," added Shamar. He also wondered if White Boy Ty had anything to do with it.

"I'm pretty sure that's already situated."

"I hope so."

Dejah nodded. "Me too," she said. A pause ensued between them, then she said, "There's something I wanna share wit' you, cuz, and I want your honest opinion on it."

"There's no other way to give it."

That's when she told him about Heaven's demands to have Rikah brough to her. For several days now, Dejah had been sitting on this matter. She wasn't sure how she wanted it to play out without causing a ruckus.

"Mookie," said Shamar

Again, Dejah nodded her head. It turned out that Mookie and Rikah were a couple, and that posed a major problem. Mookie could get quite lethal when crossed. She was unpredictable.

"It's gonna happen regardless, whether we give her up or not, cuz," said Shamar. "Hev would just send somebody up here to do it themselves. And if she has to do that herself, after bringing it to your attention first, then you already know how she's gonna look at you from now on."

"And you, too, Shamar."

"Which means?"

"We give her what she wants," said another voice. Both Dejah and Shamar looked up to see Pepper shutting the rear glass patio door. "And who are we talkin' about exactly? Or am I interfering now?"

Pepper was part of the team now, although she could be a bit aggravating at times, she was cool people. Her uncle, Savage Joe, had been forthcoming with his resources and a for sure connection in the underworld. The old man was a street legend, and apparently, he'd already taken a liking to Delani, who was out there making major moves for the team. The murder of Damian sealed the deal, and now the crew was seeing some great things sprout from it. And Pepper would not let them forget it. She was determined.

"Then I guess it's back to trying to figure this shit out on my own," Pepper said.

"What did you need, Pepper?" Dejah gave her cousin a patient hand and turned her attention on the other woman.

"That package has arrived just now," said Pepper. She was a jet black, chubby female with dazzling eyes and pretty as a kiss. Pepper had a thing for Shamar, but he acted like he never noticed it.

Hearing this perked Dejah up a little. "Okay. I'll be in there after I'm done with Shamar. Thanks, Pep." With a lingering glance down at Shamar, hoping to catch his eye, Pepper turned back for the glass sliding door and went back inside.

Dejah said something under her breath.

"What?" Shamar questioned her.

"I said, it may do you some good to show her at least a little attention, Shamar."

Shamar looked at her like she was crazy. "You would say something like that."

"It's beneficial."

"For who? You?" he retorted.

"For us," she replied. "The team"

"But aren't we already benefiting through Pepper, cuz? What more do we need to do?"

"Seeing her happy is what her uncle, Savage Joe, wants, no matter what the situation may be. And if that happiness pertains to something you can do to keep it that way, then you need to run that game accordingly. I mean, your feelings don't have to be involved, Shamar," said Dejah as she leaned in towards him. "We tryna win right now, and in order to do that, we must ultimately utilize whatever advantage we have to sell that shit."

"In so many words, pimp that bitch?"

Dejah smirked and nodded "Exactly."

Reluctantly, Shamar nodded his head and tried not to think about Danielle back home. He loved and missed his wifey deeply, and he, no doubt, knew she felt the same.

Then his thoughts went back to the initial matter at hand. Rikah. It was Shamar who had recruited Rikah. He saw something in her that most people had overlooked. She had turned out to be everything he'd ever hoped for in a team player.

"I'll deal wit' Rikah on my own terms," he told her. After she shot Heaven that night, Shamar had sent for Rikah. She had come faithfully, like the loyal goon she was. Now Shamar had to honor the game and respect it for what it was.

He had to give Heaven what she wanted.

Fuck what they been through.

Heaven was his truest of them all.

So Rikah had to go.

No exceptions.

Chapter 20

Delani looked absolutely uncomfortable as he stood there with his arms outstretched at his sides. A duo of tailors were measuring his lengths in preparation to fit him for a selection of tailor made customed suits. As he stood there, getting tape measured and fitted. Delani looked from the two certified tailors to Savage Joe, who looked back at him as a proud father would his son.

"To be the man, Delani, you have to look the part," said the older gangster, who was already dressed in a five-thousand-dollar Tom Ford three-piece suit. The man looked, smelled and even acted like money.

Savage Joe had been the best friend of Anthony Mendoza, the son of a legendary mob boss, who was murdered in his own home, some thirty years ago. The Mendoza family was one of the most notorious, dangerous and feared families in all of Harlem, New York. They ran a successful drug operation along with a few upscale diners and casinos that brought in a lucrative exchange.

Before Anthony was murdered, he was the reputed don, the head honcho, whose position was handed down to him five years prior by his father, Ricardo Mendoza, who died of heart failure. Unfortunately, Anthony had been set up for the kill by his mistress, Gabrielle Savino, a distant relative of one of Anthony's longtime foes. At one point, the honorable Lucci Family, who was a faithful ally to the Mendoza Family, stepped in to assist in locating the perpetrators to avenge Anthony's death. But by this time, Joseph Green had already taken it upon himself to hunt the killers down. He knew things that only Anthony confided in him. With that information, he found his killers and murdered them all in the most savage way possible. Thus, he got the name Savage Joe, and from that point on, he was loved and respected even more in the underworld, from which his status evolved.

"Last time I wore a suit was to my fifth-grade graduation," said Delani, once the tailors had what they needed to get started.

"Well," Savage Joe beckoned him over to sit with him on the bench he was occupying. "Consider this a higher graduation process from being a street thug to a boss," he replied.

"I've been a boss," said Delani.

That made the big man laugh. "I'm sure you were, son, but this is a whole nother level."

"What's in the bag?" Dalani nodded in the direction of a dark colored gift bag, resting at the older man's calfskin loafers, on the floor. He had watched the interaction of one of his two bodyguards entering the tailor shop deliver the bag. Delani had a feeling what the bag contained wasn't an ordinary gift, but something of more sustenance.

It was just like Savage Joe to conduct the most important business in places one would never expect.

To answer his question, Savage Joe reached down for the bag and sat it on the bench between them. He then told Delani to reach into the bag and take out what was inside.

"A book?" thought Delani, once he was told, and sure enough, it was a book indeed.

"But not just any book, son," Savage Joe saw the questioning look Delani shot him. "The title of that book is what, Delani?" he asked him.

Delani gazed down upon the book and read that the title said, "Mind is the Master."

"By James Allen," said Joe. "A great thinker indeed."

"Okay," Delani stretched the word to indicate that he needed further elaboration.

"I want you to read that book and dissect it, Delani. But not just only that, open it up and scan between the pages."

Opening the book as directed, Delani noticed something other than just the original pages that were part of the book. Also included within the middle of those pages were pages of what appeared to be a ledger.

"What you see are actual pages to a ledger," said Savage Joe.

"You know what a ledger is, right?"

Hesitantly, Delani nodded his head, "Yeah."

"Well, this ledger once belonged to a dear friend of mine, who passed away four weeks ago. Inside is information that could get you and your whole family wiped out off the face of this earth, son."

He let that simmer for a brief moment.

"In the process of dissecting the book, I want you to also dissect the ledger as well. Utilize it and do as you should with it. There, you'll find a lot of debts that need to get paid at once. For every debt paid, you take thirty percent off the top and bring me the rest. Understand?"

Another nod from Delani.

"I need a verbal answer, Delani. A nod of the head at this rate could get your killed."

"I understand," he answered.

"And you are not to participate in any of the street dealings. Assemble yourself a loyal and thorough team, which I'm sure you have already, and command that team, without getting personally involved. Again you are top level boss status now," said Joe. "There's no need for you to get your hands dirty. Understood?"

"Clearly," said Delani.

"Good. Nice. Now let's talk about trust," Savage Joe suggested, with a quick gesture of the hand to inform Delani to dispose of the book.

But Delani no longer wanted to talk, he wanted to get down to business. He didn't need a book to determine how he should conduct his business. And besides, he didn't want to hurt the old man's feelings, by telling him that he once owned that very same book back when he was on lock. He read and dissected the book twice already.

Delani was already on top of his game. The older gangster underestimated him, probably due to his age. But he had another thing coming when he finally saw that Delani was built for this shit.

He was destined.

Later that afternoon, when his time with Savage Joe was spent and worthwhile, Delani made his way back to the mansion, where he and Dejah sat in her home office to talk privately.

"What do you think?" he asked her, after he gave her the rundown on his time with Savage Joe. "I want you to keep it all the way real."

"That's the only way I can keep it, Dee," she replied. "You're the chosen one."

"The chosen one?" he muttered.

"Of all the people he could have chosen for this role, he chose you, Delani. And I'm talkin' about decades of loyalty and trustin' in those who helped him become the man he is today. He went over them to entrust this position to you. So, own it. You don't need my opinion, nigga," she spoke confidently.

No reply.

"Are you nervous?" she asked.

Delani admitted, "A little," and then he let out a heavy breath. "But I can do it."

"I know you can."

He shrugged. "The chosen one, huh?" Delani dropped his head for a brief moment, lifted his head back up, and Dejah would have sworn she saw worry in his eyes.

He was worried. Because there was no turning back now that he had given Savage Joe his word.

His word was bond, even with the possibility of dying in the process.

Chapter 21

As the bathroom sink water ran continuously, Heaven bit into a towel and sobbed in agony. She had been putting up a front this whole time. When in solace alone, she succumbed to the misery that she was really enduring inside.

"My head hurts," Heaven cried like a brokenhearted child in that bathroom. The pain in her head was excruciating, she just wanted it to stop. "My head hurts, so bad," she wept.

It was nine days after Toby's escape. Nine days of fighting the urge to give up, to take her pain out on somebody else. But just when she was on the verge of doing just that, her position as a mother stopped her. If not for herself, she certainly had to be strong for her daughter.

Heaven was going through it.

She was in pain, physically and emotionally. Heaven had never in her life hurt like this before. Well, except for when she found out her father had been murdered. But then again, that was a whole different type of pain she had felt. That pain brought on so much other pain that the suffering was still existent.

There was a knock at the door. Heaven slowly, righted herself and stood up from the lid of the toilet. She shut off the water faucet and refused to look at herself in the mirror. She definitely would not like the sight. She knew she looked terrible, maybe even scary.

Gone was the wraparound bandage on her head, but a smaller one yet remained, until the bullet wound fully healed. The wound was on the side of her head, near the temple area. It had to be God's doing to let her survive a shot to the head and to the torso, while having a seizure at the same time. Heaven was destined to live, she had a true purpose in her life.

With her IV-stroller in hand, Heaven unlocked the door to find her uncle, Chad, standing there. He had a look on his face as if he was contemplating busting the door down to get in to her.

"What are you doing here, Chad?"

"To see you, what else?" he said simply. Then he took her by the arm to attempt to escort her back to her bed, until she shrugged him away.

"I'm not an invalid, Chad," she said harshly.

"I was just tryna help, niece," Chad shrugged his shoulders and jammed both hands into the pockets of his jeans. He then glanced over at LaShonda and his aunt, LaVetra, and knew by their gazes he should just respect her mind.

Heaven climbed back onto the side of her bed to sit down and looked up at Chad. "Sorry for yelling at you, Chad. I'm just tired of everybody treatin' me like I'm fuckin' delicate or something. I'm not gonna break. If that's the case, I wouldn't be here right now."

"I understand," he sighed.

She said, "Now what took your big head butt so long to see me?"

Chad had moved away from Quincy to raise his family somewhere safer than his hometown. He relocated to Jasper, Florida, where he worked as a contractor for a construction company. His latest job was a remodel of a five-star hotel that was damaged by fire.

"It's all good," said Heaven. "You've made it back. That's all that matters."

The tension subsided and both uncle and niece talked and kicked it, along with the others.

Then the door opened, and Jamir entered the room with a cellphone to his ear. "Hold on, brah, here she go right here," said Jamir. Before approaching Heaven and giving her the phone, he switched it over to video call, so she could see who it was on the other end.

When Heaven received the phone and saw that it was Shamar, her heart raced with joy. "Shamar," she cried out.

"Really?" LaShonda leapt to her feet and hurried over to the bed. "Lemme see him, Hev."

Heaven showed her, and Jamir watched his mother squeal with happiness at the sight of his brother.

"Please tell me you're wit—"

LaShonda and was cut off by the shake of Shamar's head. "Nobody knows I'm taking this call right now, Mama. We gon' keep it like that, alright?" Shamar replied.

LaShonda nodded. "Okay," she said. But she was still overjoyed to see him, and Shamar reassured her that everybody was progressing, despite the circumstances.

"I'm glad to hear that," said LaVetra. "Progress."

It was then that Shamar asked to speak with Heaven privately. With Jamir's help, she reentered the bathroom, avoiding Chad's piercing gaze, as he watched.

"Stay wit' me, Jay," said Heaven after they had gone inside and he turned to leave.

He shut the door and locked it.

"We good, Hev?"

"Yeah."

"A'ight. I had received word that you want Rikah brought to you," said Shamar.

Both Heaven and Jamir looked at each other and then turned their eyes back to the phone.

"Yeah," said Heaven in a quiet voice.

And that's when the screen of the phone veered in the image of what appeared to be an unconscious Rikah lying upon what looked like the floor of a basement or something. Apparently, Rikah had to be put down and out in order for them to reach this point. That's when the image of an assault rifle was pressed against Rikah's head. Heaven gasped at the realization of what she was witnessing.

"When you say do it, it's done," said Shamar.

"No," Heaven blurted out.

"No?"

"I said no, Shamar. Do not kill her." Heaven shut her eyes for a brief moment. She was wrestling with mixed emotions. Here she had the power to pay Rikah back for what she did, but then she heard LaVetra's voice in her head, warning her about forgiveness.

Forgiving those who harmed you was a very hard pill to swallow for Heaven.

"I forgive her," said Heaven.

"You what?" Shamar was baffled by this. "After what she did to you, you forgive her? Then why the fuck you had me go through all this shit for?" he frowned.

"To tell her face to face, Shamar."

"Did that bullet to your head make you soft or something, Hev?"

"Watch your mouth, Mar," interjected Jamir.

A lone tear fell from Shamar's right eye, and he said, "It's too late to forgive now. I can't do that. That's not how this shit goes, Hev."

"Shamar, no," screamed Heaven.

But it was too late, for Shamar had already given the signal. And right there on the screen, they watched as a series of slugs punched Rikah in the head, spraying blood and brains in the process.

All Jamir could do was gape in shock. Shamar murdered his own.

Mercilessly.

And then the call was disconnected.

He was gone.

"That wasn't Shamar," said Heaven, softly pressing her back against the wall and closing her eyes.

Jamir looked at her for a long moment. "What do you mean that wasn't him?"

"The Shamar we know woulda respected my mind."

No reply.

"He's changed," Heaven exclaimed as she opened her eyes to look at her brother. "And I got a feeling our brotha has changed for the worse."

Chapter 22

The last thing White Boy Ty wanted was to reveal to the enemy that he had a daughter. He didn't want to risk that happening, which was why he kept Shamoorah out in the country parts of the St. John area, away from the constant bullshit going on in town. Plus, Uncle Bart was enjoying his new role of playing uncle to Shamoorah and Nikitta. It was understood that his protective nature was in dire need now. Doing whatever it took to protect his household was what Bart did best. Not saying that Shamoorah couldn't hold her own, but it was always good to know that help was near.

Uncle Bart would not let harm come to them. He was an old legend. One of the last of a dying breed. But that still didn't stop White Boy Ty from spending time with his beloved daughter, and of course Shamoorah.

Like now, he had just taken them both shopping, with Abigail tagging along, to the Tallahassee Mall, where they had a joyful experience. It felt damn good to do something normal for a change, and he had Shamoorah to thank for that.

After spending a couple hours in the mall, they went out for ice cream for another treat for Nikita. Then Ty suggested that he stop by his condo that he and Toby had leased together, before shit went south. He wanted to check on a few things before heading back to Quincy, and the quiet world out in the country parts.

Shamoorah couldn't get enough of the country life. She was brought up as a pure blooded city girl. She never even knew that you could eat raccoon and possum and rabbit, until she met Uncle Bart. They went fishing together two days ago and Shamoorah damn near lost her mind when she reeled in a fourteen-inch mangrove snapper fish, or as the old country folk call them, "black snapper." The big catch almost traumatized the poor girl.

"Gotta get you out here more often, missy," Bart had told her.

When they pulled up at the Crestview Condominiums and parked inside the parking garage, which was on the level with the assigned residence, away from the outside activities, Ty was hesitant with asking Shamoora to join him. He didn't want to feel like he would be violating the space that he and Toby shared together.

"Good. Cause I gotta change Nikita's diaper anyway," said Shamoorah, not thinking much of the concept of White Boy Ty living with another female.

Nikita fussed that she wanted Ty to hold her, and despite the fact that she was arid, he carried her all the way up to the fifth floor apartment with pleasure. Once inside, Nikita was handed back to her mother and Ty directed her to the bathroom.

"Nice place you got here," complimented Abigail, as she marveled over its creative decor and the fine taste of its mixed flavors of interior designs.

"It was home," he said.

"Isn't it still?" She asked curiously. "I mean, I understand your situation, but you're just gonna let this place exist alone now, and not utilize the space?"

Before he could answer, there was a knock at the front door, making them both look in its direction.

"You even have visitors still," said Abigail.

"Shut up, Abigail," Ty told her and marched back towards the front door. He already knew who it was, which was none other than Charlotte Castillo from down the hall, the incredible cosmetics brand manager. Her and Toby had become fast associates, before White Boy Ty knew that she even existed.

But when he opened the door and didn't find Charlotte on the other side, but someone he least expected, Ty frowned.

"Debra," he said in an earnest tone.

"Somebody doesn't look happy to see me, after all I had to go through to rescue your other half," Debra Moretti said, before patting a delicate hand upon his check and easing by him into the apartment.

"What did you do wit' Toby?"

"She's safe, Ty," the italian matriarch spoke up. Today she was dressed in a simple pair of Khaki pants and a pear-colored blouse. "But aren't you suspicious that your place could be bugged, Ty?"

"Why would it be bugged?" he asked her, concerned.

"Why would it not be?" she asked.

Ty seemed to think about that for a second.

"Don't fret, I saw to the matter already," she replied, and then said, "II had the place swept and collected all of them for you. You'll be happy to find them fried and crispy in your microwave.

It took him a moment for her words to register. then he left her standing there, as he headed for the spacious kitchen. At the same time, Debra turned her gaze on Abigail and gave her a curious glance.

"You have pretty eyes," she replied.

"Thank you," said Abigail. "And you are?"

Debra didn't even hesitate introducing herself, which left Abigail still in wonder as to why she was there and what her business was with Ty.

When Ty returned, all he could do was shake his head. He said, "How did you know?"

"You just can never be too careful, Ty."

He nodded without a reply.

"She's in New Orleans. I put her in a safe house with round-the-clock security and medical personnel. Toby is very safe there, so don't go plundering. Okay?" said Debra, exchanging a knowing look with Ty. That's when Shamoorah entered the room and both women looked at each other in silent curiosity.

There was so much more White Boy Ty wanted to ask the Italian woman, but decided not to, not in front of Shamoorah. He did not want to expose to her anything more than what she was already aware of.

"Lemme holla at you in the back for a minute," said Ty. He stood there waiting for Debra to move, then he cast a solemn glance in Shamoorah's direction as they exited the room together.

Moments later, Ty had led her into what he transformed into a game room. It had a pool table, an entertainment center, which had a 107-inch flat screen Plasma TV and a large assortment of video games. The spacious room had a minibar, theater lounge chairs, and even a professional punching bag in the far corner, next to a floor-to-ceiling mahogany framed mirror.

"This is neat," said Debra animatedly.

"As if you haven't already seen every square inch of the place," he retorted.

"I haven't."

Ty looked at her pensively.

"That's what I have loyal henchmen for, Ty."

"Anyway." Ty gave her a dismissive gesture. "How can I be sure that Toby is really safe?"

"You'll just have to trust me."

"I don't even know you!"

"All the reason for you to get to know me," she told him. "Starting with what I have for you right here." Ty watched as she reached into the inside pocket of her woman's blazer and brought out a thin manila envelope.

"What's this?" Ty reluctantly accepted the envelope.

"Open it," she encouraged.

When Ty opened the envelope and peered inside, there contained two photos, which he reached to grab. The first photo was all he needed to see to make him gasp and his heart begin to quicken. Then he looked up at her in surprise.

Then that surprise turned to fear.

A fear that would no doubt give him reason to do nothing but trust her.

Chapter 23

It had been almost three weeks since Veronica died. Then the death of her big brother, leaving just their mother, Tabitha to drown in misery and endless bottles of Jack Daniels. Their funerals were something like a blur in Heaven's mind. The details of their home-going were hazy at best. Heaven remembered being there at the funeral, her best friend's final journey, but to her it seemed like an out of body experience.

She and Monique talked almost every day, just like they always had, just to make sure one another was okay. But Heaven spent most of her time in therapy, trying to get herself back in tip-top shape again.

Meanwhile, Jamir, Tilly and Marco were holding the fort down for the team. There was money that still needed to be made. But, due to the latest killings in town, the law was making it hard for them to do so. So instead, the team utilized the time to focus more on their own personal plans and goals.

It had been bartender June and Jamir's idea to improve the community spirit of Gadsden County by organizing a town makeover, during the Labor Day Weekend, for the youths, for the community.

Both combined crews, HCG and Royal Mafia, pooled their resources and funded the whole event. They went around all the town area, refurbishing all neighborhood parks with newer basketball goals and nets, repairing all the swing sets, fences, repaving the worn cracked- basketball courts that needed restoration. Then Lele somehow managed to organize a neighborhood dance out at the Complex, over the near Lake Skillet area. The whole weekend was turnt up and all went surprisingly well.

Even Heaven had come out to show her face, before heading back out to go do her thing.

"We want some life about the town again," said the Reverend Tommy Gordon, who had shown up to assist. "Where the youngins have nothing done for them, they migrate to other places lookin' for peace and fun."

"Aye, well, there's youngsters and then there's the young people, if you know what I mean," said Mr. Levi Ross, a school teacher.

The reverend nodded.

"Alot of these youngsters like to travel round town and disrupt things, killin one another, fightin' and the likes. I could name quite a few of our own, who're never satisfied unless they're causing hell round here."

Reverend Gordon gave him a stern look.

"Excuse my choice of phrase, Rev," said Ross. "But you get where I'm coming from, right?"

"Of course, I do."

Right then, both Zamon and Vonte walked up and came to rest before the two men. At this approach, Mr. Levi Ross took a cautionary step back, as he watched both hooliganz attentively.

"Mr. Ross," Zamon had a devilish grin on his face. "I got somethin' I wanna tell you," he said.

Suspicion was writing all over Ross's face as Vonte too was grinning with mischief.

"What is it?"

That's when Zamon's face turned serious and he then extended his hand towards the older man. This was Zamon's former seventh grade Social Studies teacher. The man looked like he was in pain before he reluctantly took Zamon's hand.

"I just wanna say I'm sorry for all the shit I took you through at school. You a good man, Mr Ross. No doubt." Zamon then snatched the teacher into a brief embrace.

"Well," said Ross. "I didn't expect that one."

"What did you expect?"

"Some trickery of some sort," grinned the teacher, now relaxed a little after suspecting mischief.

The reverend smirked.

"There's a season for everythang, Mr. Ross. A time to play and a time for redemption."

"I hear that," interjected Rev. Gordon.

"Good day, fellaz." Zamon saluted the two older men as he and Vonte swaggered away to go mingle with the community.

"You see," replied the reverend with a slap on the other man's shoulder. "And then you have some who actually have the courage to change."

Not long after the hooliganz had left, Mr. Ross was startled by a kick in the back of the leg. The impact caused the older man to bend at the knee, off balance. Then he turned around to spot two younger kids dashing away laughing.

That's when the reverend saw it, the Post-it sticky note on the back of the teacher's shirt. Then he reached up and snatched the sticky note away to show his companion.

"Then again," he said, "maybe not."

Kick Me is what was drawn on the sticky note in big, bold, black wording.

All Mr. Ross could do was shake his head.

Then he laughed at himself.

"Sucker," grinned the reverend and, once again, slapped the other man across the shoulder.

The rest of the evening went swell, giving the community something to be proud of. There was no bad blood in the air, at least not during the events, and a change in the atmosphere was all that was needed. Later that night, the whole team retired to the bar up on the block, having a night cap. There were about a hundred of them present. Lately, there hadn't been any recruiting, the team was just focused on growing and appreciating what they already had.

During the moment, Heaven had appeared amongst her family and ordered everybody's attention. Standing next to her on either side was Tilly and Jamir, both presenting stone-hard expressions.

"At this time, Royal Mafia no longer exists," Heaven announced in a firm tone.

Some whispers and grumbling among the group transpired before silence was ordered, once again. This time it was Tilly who spoke up.

"Royal Mafia is dead," she said. "Everybody in this room are all Hooliganz Crime Gang affiliates. We are one whole and one family now."

"One whole, one family," added Heaven.

"One whole, one family," Jamir repeated, and saw several of his brothers nod their approval.

"You will still keep your assigned positions," Heaven said to her former Royals." But we're about to do things a little different this time," she proclaimed.

"Different how?" asked Bayina

And that's when Debra Moretti was let into the big room and took her stance next to Heaven. With her presence came a level of respect from Tilly and the majority of the other former Royals in the room. It was known that Debra had taken it upon herself to save Toby, and for that, their love and respect came without effort.

Then Heaven gestured for Debra to take the floor, so that she could properly introduce herself to all.

"Drugs will be no longer our only source of income to build from," said Heaven.

"So, what does she have to offer?" said Kweli.

Debra told them exactly that. What she had to offer was something beyond the obvious.

It was powerful.

Chapter 24

His name was Khalid Abdul-Lateef, a dedicated young Muslim and Associate professor of world languages multi-cultural and Gender Studies at Imam University. Hollow had the Muslim bio down cold. There was confidence in the way Khalid moved that he, Hollow, the latest recruit of Shamar's, recognized instantly. At 7:02 p.m. Khalid Abdul-Lateef had left his private apartment in Queens for his inconspicuous black and red Dodge Challenger and rode in silence until he reached the three-star restaurant, not too far from the Upper East Side, where he also privately owned a popular gentlemen's club.

Once at the restaurant, it was then that Hollow and his crew noticed that the Muslim was also accompanied by a full security detail that actually gave him free rein to move as he pleased, without causing too much attention. Here, he was escorted discreetly into the restaurant to where the maître d' then escorted him to his reserved table in the back.

Two of his three men sat at a neighboring table in the room, with the third man just beyond the exit door, near the front of the main dining room. The three men around Khalid did not make eye contact with him, nor he with them. There was little acknowledgement between Khalid and his protectors, and no real conversation whatsoever. They had an arrangement that no one in the loop seemed anxious to rectify.

It wasn't long before the entrance door opened and in swooped a beautiful, tall female with a little curly haired boy in hand. Upon seeing her enter the restaurant Khalid grinned broadly and rose to his feet. Her name was Grace Newberry, she was twenty-nine, positively old for a model, although she was one of the most beautiful women Hollow had ever seen, a tough challenge, even on the runway full of striking models.

"That snow bunny sexy as fuck," said Hollow to his right hand man, Kreature, sitting beside him.

Kreature just nodded, without a reply. He was a nigga of little words and nothing but action.

In the restaurant, Khalid embraced the woman first, then he lifted up the little boy and kissed his face. This was the Muslim's family away from his family back over in Las Vegas, where he lived. He was one of the marks in the ledger that Delani was about to have dealt with accordingly.

"Get in position," said Hollow. Without a word still, Kreature reached for his phone to correspond via text message with the team of shooters that were also already waiting on standby for the command.

Shit was about to go down.

Back in the restaurant, the small, private family was seated around the table, talking amongst themselves, while Grace studied the menu before her. The little boy looked like he'd rather be at home on his Xbox 360, munching on Oreo cookies, than being there right now.

"They're in position," said Kreature. "Make the call."

Hollow punched in the number to make the call and watched from his vantage point as Khalid paused in mid reach for his glass of champagne. The Muslim glanced down at his two-thousand-dollar Canali wool, silk and cashmere Kei coat and reached into his side pocket for his phone. When he looked at the number on the screen, he didn't recognize it, but he deemed it important because he wasted no time answering it.

"Hello. Who is this?" he demanded.

Hollow snapped into his role.

"I want you to take a good look at the woman and the little boy in front of you," he said.

From the distance, Khalid scrunched up his face in open disdain, but he did look over at his family and got the shock of his life. Both Grace and the little boy, Kamal, were totally oblivious of the inferred beams dancing across their faces from some unseen weapon.

"Please don't do this, what is it that you want?" Khalid replied in a panicked but low tone.

"I come in regards of Jimmy Medina."

At hearing the name, the Muslim's whole body tensed up. "Um, isn't Jimmy deceased?"

"Yes, he is," said Hollow. "But that doesn't stop what is about to happen, if you don't cooperate."

"And that is what exactly?"

"It's pay up time, homeboy," said Hollow.

Silence.

Hollow said, "You owe Jimmy seven hundred and fifty thousand dollars. But since you wanna play dumb, make that shit a million even.

"A mil?" The Muslim reeled back in shock.

"I'm texting you the information right now. You got fifteen minutes to make the wire transfer."

"Fifteen minutes?" Khalid cried out. "How can I do that in such short time?" he stressed.

"You find a way to do everything else, you'll figure it out. Oh, and please tell your men to stay put before that bitch brains explode out the back of her muthafuckin' head," sneered Hollow darkly.

Khalid glanced towards Tarek, the leader of his security detail, sitting alone at a nearby table by the door of the dining room. He had certainly witnessed the exchange from across the room, Khalid knew, because Tarek did not miss much.

Tarek was rising out of his seat when he noticed red dots moving along the faces of his boss and his family. With a hand signal, the other two men got up and Khalid shot up to his feet to confer with them. It only took a few words from the boss to send his men back to their seats. The looks on their faces were far from comfortable. They were all sitting ducks to an unknown enemy.

"Okay." Khalid was perspiring like crazy as he made his way back to his table.

"What is happening, Hakeem?" asked a very concerned Grace, who now was aware of the danger lurking around them.

The Muslim paid her no mind as he made the necessary calls he needed to make to execute the transfer.

"Hakeem?" Grace called him by the fake name he had given her over three years ago, when they first met on a flight from Paris to New York.

"Just humble yourself, Grace."

"You're not even humble," she spat right back.

"I'm perfectly humble," he told her when he finally connected with his financial advisor.

Outside in the car, both Hollow and Kreature watched the panicked faces of Khalid and his people. Hollow wondered if the Muslim could really make the transfer in time. This was a big step up from robbin' jewelry stores and petty drug dealers.

This was the big leagues.

This mission would grant him two hundred fifty thousand dollars more, on top of the money he was previously paid by Delani. Easy money. He could do this shit with his eyes closed. Forty-two seconds before the deadline, the money was successfully transferred to the secured account. When Delani was phoned to verify the transaction and he confirmed it, Hollow gave the final order.

"Shoot," he announced.

Seconds later, Khalid's head snapped back from the punch of a.224 round to the forehead. Then his three goons got the same treatment, dropping them like a bad habit where they stood.

Thirty minutes later, the kill team was lounging around in one of Hollow's spots, over in Brooklyn, when Delani made his presence known. Dressed in expensive Italian linen and fifteen-hundred-dollar Di Bianco calfskin bluchers shoes, Delani stepped through the door of the apartment, carrying a leather duffle bag.

"Nothin' in life is a given," said Delani, before tossing the hefty bag over to Hollow. "Everythang is meant to be earned, therefore you are deserving of what you got right now."

"For sho, bro. No doubt," said Hollow. He didn't have to look in the bag to know that a quarter million was residing inside.

That's when he gave them another name and the file to which Hollow would read up on. Two weeks was the time frame, but Hollow assured him that it could be done within a week.

"You would want to read that file first because there's no room for mistakes, Hollow."

"And I don't plan on makin' em either."

"Read," Delani said. "That's priority."

And then he was gone.

Just like that. No hanging out. Get in and get gone.

Chapter 25

It was a month and a half later, about twenty minutes after Toby decided to lay it down for the night when it happened. At first, Toby thought she was dreaming when she heard a faint noise. But after it resounded again in the quiet house, it brough her to sitting upright in her queen size bed. Somebody was inside the house. And not with her consent because she lived in the house alone.

Somebody had stealthily broken into the house somehow and was going out of their way to do it quietly. Toby was always a light sleeper. It didn't take much for her to hear anything suspicious, now that the loss of an eye seemed to have heightened her sense of hearing. The house was equipped with a security alarm system, like many others were. Toby didn't want to risk the authorities being alerted by its glitchy system and they come knocking on her front door. The last thing Toby needed was to have to deal with NOPD for any reason.

New Orleans police could be quite persistent when they wanted to get their point across, and brutal, as well. Pretty much, any other typical black-dominated areas that has claimed the Murder Capital status in its time. Toby didn't want to go through that headache, which was why she reached for her .9mm Beretta instead of her phone to call for help. The only thing she was gonna be calling was the shots from her gun at whoever the fool was who violated her space.

She eased out of the bed and padded quietly over to the door. With just as much ease, she was out of the door into the hallway. The house was dead silent, except for the very faint noise coming from the kitchen area. The culprit was very meticulous with not trying to be heard, which meant they were taking their precious time to precisely do what they came to do.

Toby thanked the spirit gods for giving her the ability to detect trouble when it was near. It also bothered her to know, if otherwise, she would have still been asleep and possibly dead before she even realized her life was in danger.

The question was how many. So far, she sensed just one person involved. This was a first for her. No one had ever broken into her house before. But there was a first time for everything, even if that meant having someone in the process.

A gun shot could ruin everything. Toby was already aware of her neighbors' suspicions of who she was and what she was doing there. They wondered why she never came out of the house and did normal things that normal people do. One shot from her gun was all it would take for her neighbors to alarm the police, just to see what happened next.

That would ruin everything. Then Toby would have to shoot them next, and then leave and never come back. It was going down in the kitchen. Someone was in her kitchen. Gong through- her fridge? After the thought crossed her mind, the flow of light peeking out from the kitchen doorway suddenly was shut off.

"Shit," came the startled reply the moment Toby stepped in the doorway just as they were stepping out.

"The fuck you doing?" barked Toby. Then she doubled-over in instant discomfort after receiving a punch to the stomach. Her unknown assailant then took off running in the dark house. Toby wanted to put a bullet in them but instead took chase.

Unfortunately, the perpetrator didn't go back in the direction which they came, because it damn sure wasn't the front door, with its triple-secured lock source. But that's exactly where they ran to, not knowing that they'd run into their own trap. That was where Toby bashed them in the back of the head with her gun, while they were trying desperately to escape through the front door with its lock system. The padlock and the security chain is what did it. There wasn't enough time.

Too late.

Apparently, the blow to the back of the head had knocked them out. They lay slumped right there on the floor in front of the door. When Toby reached to turn on the light, she could not believe what lie before her eyes.

"Damn," she muttered. He was just a scrawny little black boy, probably no older than ten. He was dressed in worn, torn, dirty clothes and a pair of busted up Reeboks that were obviously too big for his small feet. Also, strapped over both bony little shoulders in front of him was a backpack. Toby didn't need to look inside to know what the backpack actually contained.

What she did want to know was who this kid was and why he broke into her home, only to steal food from her kitchen. Toby could already see it in her mind's eye, this little nigga was about to affect her deeply.

Minutes later, after tying his arms behind his back, Toby smacked him a few times to bring him back around.

"Why you keep hittin' me?" the boy groaned.

"You hit me, muthafucka!"

He groaned again, but louder this time. When he tried to sit up and realized his arms were bound, he went into panic-mode.

"Please don't call the bad boyz on me. I can't go to jail," the boy whined.

"You should," Toby told him grimly.

"No!"

106

"Gimme one reason why you shouldn't?" Toby squatted down next to his dry peezy head.

The boy seemed to think about that for a second. He looked up at her and noticed that she had one eye. The one-look freaked him out a little. But there was something else he saw in Toby, that somehow gave him the courage to want to confide in her.

"My two sistaz," he said. "I'm all they got. I'm the man of the house. They need me there to protect them." There were tears in his eyes and Toby found herself being softened by his grief.

"What's your name, lil man?"

He hesitated. "Kordae?"

"How old are you, Kordae?"

"Twelve."

"Twelve?" Toby shook her head sadly. "And how old are your two sistaz, Kordae?"

"Five," he said. "They are twins."

How ironic is that, thought Toby as Vermani and Delani came to mind. She had already fallen for one set of twins, and now here it was, the universe was about to introduce her to another pair.

"What's their names?" she wanted to know.

Kordae didn't hesitate this time. "Nakia and Tamia. I left them at the house to go find 'em somethin' to eat. They hungry," he said anxiously.

"By breakin' in other people's houses? What if you had gotten shot and died, lil nigga? Who was gonna look after your sistaz then?"

"Nobody," Kordae looked hurt to say that.

"Where are your parents at?"

Kordae said, "Mama left the house a week ago and neva came back. My daddy is dead. My sistaz daddy ain't shit. I'm all they got."

That's when Toby made her decision and released him from his binds. "You got me now," she said and shook her head. Then she reached down to help him up to his feet.

"Where your sistaz at? Where is home?"

When he told her he lived in the Seventh Ward area, Toby had settled her nerves. She herself lived in the Lower Ninth Ward, over cross the canal. To know that Kordae had to come way over to the Ninth Ward to earn his keep only told Toby one thing, she was not dealing with the average twelve-year-old kid.

"Let's go get your sistaz," she said as she stood up and faced him head on.

"And bring them here? To this house?"

"Where else, nigga?"

Suddenly, he broke out in a sheepish grin. "You gonna take care of us now?"

"Do I have a fuckin' choice, Kordae?"

"Yeah," he nodded. "You actually do."

Toby had a strong feeling that Kordae was about to make her out to be something she wouldn't have ever imagined being in a million years. The little nigga was playing on her soft spot. She was a sucker for kids.

Chapter 26

The 2019 cocaine white Range Rover pulled to a halt outside the forest-green and white bungalow house on Davis Street, in the Hill Side area. Occupying the SUV was Junior Herring and three of his loyal crew members. Where they came from, the group was called Money Steppaz Gang, better known as the MSG Clique. They hailed from the south side of Orlando, a crew whose affiliation ranged from murder, fraud, and extortion to selling the best weed in the city. They had a weed connect straight out of Mexico, and it had the money coming in like clockwork.

But this was Junior's home, he was from Quincy, and his presence was long overdue. He was back where it all started. He was home.

Junior opened the door and climbed out of the Range Rover, attired in Gucci, linen and loafers. He was almost twenty years old and had come a long way from the young pushover he used to be. Leaving Quincy when he was fifteen was the best thing to ever happen to him. He had purpose now, a solid reputation, and Junior couldn't wait to emphasize it.

He headed for the front door of the house, with his crew of Steppaz in tow. Surprisingly, not many people were out that morning. Davis Street used to be lit, when he was coming up. All his old friends and neighbors were always actively doing something.

"Don't this spot remind you of Mercy Drive?" said Stank, a stocky built nigga with deep waves.

"A lil bit, tho," exclaimed Boosie.

Just before they reached the front porch, the front door of the house opened.

"Cuz!" Junior grinned upon seeing his older female cousin, Shannon, standing there in the doorway all bowlegged and jazzy in her skinny jeans and flats. It was Shannon who had summoned him back home, and Junior didn't think twice about returning.

"You finally made it," she replied, after hugging him briefly. "Yall c'mon in the house. I started hookin' you up some breakfast when you called to let me know you in town."

"Now you talkin' my language," Ratchet replied.

She grinned and turned from the door.

"Don't make me kill your ass about that one," Junior said with a straight face.

Boosie nudged his fella Steppa before entering the house.

Ratchet shrugged and followed. He was the most ruthless one of them all. Ratchet was also the little brother of two niggaz who founded Money Steppaz Gang. It was also him who befriended Junior and gave his blessings to have his friend recruited to the clique.

Since then, they had built a rapport so mean that you would think they were the actual founders. Fifteen minutes later, Shannon had the crew all sitting around the kitchen table feasting on their home cooked breakfast. Not only was Shannon an awesome hair stylist and beautician, but she was a damn good cook, too, a beast in the kitchen.

"So, who killed my uncle and cousin, cuz?" Junior asked chewing and sipping his glass of orange juice. When Shannon spun around to face him, the look on her face was grim. She didn't expect him to bring up the subject in front of the others. She also didn't want to seem vulnerable and emotionally agonized in front of the others.

"You can speak in front of my people, cus. We are all on the same team," added Junior.

"That's not my point."

"Then what's the fuckin' point, Shannon?" Junior frowned up at her and Shannon could only hope that they would not reach a disagreement over the whole situation regarding discretion.

With a deep breath, Shannon said, "All I know is that that HCG crew had somethin' to do wit' what happened to Uncle Pitt and Dyamond."

"And where is Bre?"

"You really wanna know?"

He gave her a stern expression instead.

"Bre is running wit' the same crew, Junior. Her and that bitch LeLe." Now Shannon was angry, after sharing with her cousin what was going on.

"So Lele was down wit' them muthafuckaz killin' her man, while Bre stood by and let them get away wit' killin' her own uncle and cousin?"

"But you know Bre didn't see eye to eye wit' uncle Pitt after what he did, cuz,"

"What he did?" said Stank curiously.

Several years ago, Pitt was arrested for assault and battery against his own sister, Tangi, who was pregnant in the process and had a miscarriage. After a week in jail, Tangi had recanted her statement to free her brother, because it was clear that Pitt was looking to spend the rest of his life in prison for what went down with his sister.

Bre had never forgiven Pitt for hurting her mother. She had also made attempts at doing him great bodily harm. But her mother and several more of her family members intervened, and Bre backed off.

But she didn't forget.

"It was probably her ass the one who did it," said Boosie with earnest.

Stank nodded.

LAND OF THE HOOLIGANZ 4 | IRA B

"Then she could very much die, too," said Junior. He rose from the table and exited the kitchen. His cousin looked like she wanted to follow.

"No," Rachet stopped her, "Let him have his space to think this shit over,"

Shannon hesitated, "I don't want him going out there to do-"

"Do somethin' stupid? Crazy?" Boosie cut her off and she looked at him wearily. "That's the last thang you have to worry about him doing. Brah doesn't act on his emotions, Shannon."

"That'll get you killed," said Stank.

"But we got him, baby gurl," Rachet reassured her with a brief nod. "Once he figures out what needs to be done, it's gonna get done. And trust me when I tell you this," he stood up, "you will be safe.

"Just keep your mouth shut, cuz," Stank pointed out.

"We got this," Boosie told her. "Now can I have more cheese grits and potatoes?"

Outside, leaning against the post railing on the porch, smoking a cigarette, Junior contemplated over the matters he was now faced with. He knew all about Hooliganz Crime Gang and where they originated from. He was very familiar with Shamar, who, once upon a time, bullied him on the football field during afternoon practices, all because of his interest in Heaven, whom Shamar was very protective over.

He also knew about Vermani and Delani, but it was Delani who became the more ruthless one of them all. Junior, once upon a time, wanted to join the HCG crew, just to prove he actually did have heart and could be a great team player. But he doubted Shamar, or even Delani, would agree to let him into their circle. They would have just ridiculed him instead. They thought he was a joke.

A fuckin' coward.

But little do they know, thought Junior, as he dwelled on the action he wanted to take, now that HCG had given him reason to oppose to their actions. But Junior wasn't stupid either. He was very aware of the power Hooliganz Crime Gang held in the streets. They were literally the most dangerous crew in North Florida, which meant that Junior would need more than the three Steppaz he had with him to make a statement in the streets against them. There were just too many of them. He had to call up some reinforcements.

And still, Junior knew, once action was taken, there was a possibility that he wouldn't make it out alive. But he had principles to stand on. He had vengeance to honor. He had come to set the record straight.

"Okay," he nodded his head solemnly. "Let's make it do what it do then." Junior then called for his crew and they put their heads together in preparation for war. He had a plan.

It was time to take his town back.

Chapter 27

When Nancy arrived back at her firm, after spending her morning in court warfare, she could not help but notice the flurry of activity around the frog desk on her floor. Mara, her secretary and personal assistant, was working on the computer in front of her. The printer was in high gear. Things were very active.

"What's with all this?" Nancy demanded.

"The sounds of a warrior at work," said Mara cheerfully.

"What the hell does that mean??

"Protecting the rights of the people, serving our clients, purging the judicial system of dangerous production, and bringing wrongly convicted prisoners hope."

Nancy couldn't argue with that and continued on to her office, where she shut the door and slumped down on the sofa chair against the wall. She kicked off her pumps and sighed with great relief. Before she could enjoy the comfort of her sanctuary, there was a burst of commotion outside her door. Then, all of a sudden, the door opened and in walked Nikki Graham, like she had something on her mind.

"I tried to stop her, but she wouldn't listen," Mara said from the doorway. The older woman was heated and, if she had it her way, Nikki probably would have gotten hit across her head. Nancy saw that very look in her eyes and bolted to her feet at once.

"We need to talk," Nikki announced anxiously.

"I'll take it from here, Mara. Thank you," Nancy said to her secretary.

Mara nodded quietly, shutting the door behind her, but not before shooting a piercing glare in the other woman's direction.

Afterward, Nancy turned toward Nikki and ordered her to sit down and calm her nerves. Then she moved behind her big corporate desk to have a seat herself. In the desk drawer next to her right knee was her loaded .25 automatic pistol. It sat just beneath a file folder in quick reaching distance, just in case.

"Now," she replied after opening the drawer slightly. "What seems to be the problem?"

"You know damn well what my problem is, Nancy. Let's not play these head games."

"I seriously have no clue, Nikki,"

This whole time Nikki had yet to sit down and just stood there, glaring down at the lawyer.

"I know you gave those goons my home address to use as leverage against Damian."

"I have no clue what you're talkin' about, Nikki. Why would I do something like that?

The woman sneered, "Revenge."

"For what exactly?"

"For being a sucker for love, fallin' for your own client, whose life you saved, only for him to leave you in the dust after he was released. I knew that must've made you feel so damn stupid and hurt. So much so that you used his own daughter to trap him."

To Nancy, Nikki looked like she wanted to spit in her face. She braced herself for the assault and eased her hand near the drawer with her pistol.

"Those are some serious allegations you've presented against me, Nikki. I'm quite appalled by them."

"How would you like it if it happened to you?"

"Is that a threat?"

Right then, the door opened and Delani entered the room behind Nikki Graham. In his hand, he carried a container of green grapes, strawberries and some cheese cubes that he knew the lawyer liked. Upon his entry, Nikki turned to look at him and cringed in absolute fear.

Nancy could only shake her head in discontent. This was certainly bad timing for them.

"What did I walk into just now?" he asked.

"Me being threatened by this woman, who has placed some critical allegations against me," answered Nancy. She gazed up at the other woman intently.

"Is that right?"

"No," Nikki shook her head, "I wasn't threatening her at all. I was just leaving."

But Delani was already stepping in her path to prevent her from approaching the door. The woman looked like a terrified kitten walking through a yard of sleeping pit bulls. She didn't know whether to find the nearest corner and cower, or scream for help.

She was stuck between a rock and a hard place. She felt trapped.

"Don't I know you?" he asked Nikki.

"Nope."

"You sure?" his gaze was cold.

A shiver ran down Nikki's spine. "I'm sure, sir. I don't think we've ever met."

"Do you figure we should meet?"

She shook her head no.

"I wanna know the extent of these allegations you've posed moments ago?" said Nancy.

"I apologize." Nikki turned to look at the lawyer. "It was just an honest mistake on my part. I'm going through a lot right now and it's heavy," she said in a shaky tone, as if she was on the verge of crying.

That's when Nancy got up from behind her desk to approach the frightened woman.

Delani stood firm.

"Make this the last time you step foot in my building or else you will regret it for the rest of your life, Nikki. Do I make myself clear?"

Nikki looked Nancy dead in the eyes. "You don't ever have to worry about me again. No trouble again, I apologize for the inconvenience."

"Take care of yourself, Nikki," said Delani.

The woman all but tore through the door getting out of there with them. She definitely wouldn't be coming back. And back upon the sofa Nancy went, after she relieved Delani of the containers he was still holding in his possession. She opened up one of them and plopped a few strawberries into her mouth.

"Was that fun or what?"

"No," he said.

She caught the edge in his voice.

"She was spared her life, but yet she wanted to get some type of closure?" he frowned.

"Well." Nancy shrugged. "That should be enough closure for her to stay away and quiet."

"And what if she don't?"

"She will."

"What makes you so sure of that?"

"Fear of dying and losing it all now that she knows this shit is dead for real."

"But she knew that already from the jump."

"No she didn't, sweetheart. She knew she was spared, and that was all the reason for her to risk chasing a confrontation with me to get answers."

"You only gotta say it and it's done."

She didn't respond to him.

When Delani took out his phone, she knew without a shadow of doubt what was on his mind.

"You don't really wanna do that." She laid a hand upon his arm to stop him. "Besides, she knows she's all out of chances now and won't risk talkin' about it. All she wants is to be a mother to her children, and what just happened really made her want that more now that it's clear she could die next."

Delani hesitated, then put away the phone.

"Now to what do I owe the pleasure of this unexpected visit?" Nancy replied.

"Some advice," he said.

"My specialty."

A month or so ago, Nancy had been troubled by the truth of what happened to LJ. He had died a horrible death, and she had blamed herself for it. She had been the one to lead him to his death.

Since then, Delani and his people had been of abundant support to her mental health and her career. To Delani, if it wasn't for her, he wouldn't have gained the trust of Diva and commitment to the team. Therefore, he saw to it that Nancy was taken care of on every level and had need for nothing.

They had become tight.

She was actually a cool, loyal bitch. Delani nudged her aside and dropped down on the sofa next to her. Once again, he took out his phone and showed her a photo.

"Who is she?" she asked.

"Her name is Hazel," he replied proudly. And then he told her all about the attraction.

Chapter 28

During the same moment, Taquan was opening the passenger door of his Chevy Impala for Da'Jhana to get in. He was taking her out to lunch again today. But he had to have her back before the first afternoon school period started. Education was important to her, and Da'Jhana had to make him respect that.

He wanted the best for her, and if that meant going to school too, he would definitely go.

So far, she hadn't sprouted the subject regarding his education, or else he would be joining her during school hours. But Da'Jhana also understood the importance of him being a young hooligan.

He was a street nigga, a young hustler.

Da'Jhana had been convinced that although she loved Corey, and she knew he loved her, it was Taquan she was destined to be with in the end. Taquan and her were perfect for each other.

"What you want to eat?" he asked.

"Whateva you wanna eat, babe."

A smirk crossed his face. "What I really wanna eat, I doubt you even eat," said Taquan.

"Wh-" Da'Jhana paused, let it register, and then reached out and punched him on the shoulder. "You so damn nasty, wit your freaky ass!"

"I love you, too, Daj."

Fifteen minutes later, they were sharing a table booth in McDonalds, eating chicken sandwiches and French fries. Da'Jhana could never grow tired of Micky D's, and she wasn't the actual splurging type who'd rather dine at five-star restaurants. She liked simplicity and Taquan truly appreciated that in her. But that still did not persuade him to not splurge on her, buying her nice things. She was very grateful for that as well.

After the death of her sister, a close cousin stepped up to the plate to prevent the government from putting her in the system, due to her being a minor. Her big cousin, Sammy, and his wife, Darlene, offered to take her into their home. But Da'Jhana made a big fuss about leaving her own home and fought tooth and nail to convince them she could do it on her own. Now Da'Jhana remained in the same house she grew up in, and where she lost her family. Sammy would stop by on the regular to check up on her.

Then you had the nosey, concerned neighbors of the community, having something negative to say about a sixteen-year-old girl living alone, without proper guardianship. That was all the reason for Da'Jhana to prove her worth and show them that, despite her age, a woman still lied within her, and she would no doubt conduct herself as one.

Life had brought her up hard. Da'Jhana was very wise beyond her age.

"Other than the obvious, Quan, what is your ultimate goal in life?" asked Da'Jhana with curiosity.

"Other than the obvious?"

She nodded

"I never really thought about that, bae. Being a street nigga is all I know. You know I'm the black sheep of my family, right?"

"As is majority of your homeboys."

No response.

"Being the black sheep means doing whatever to take responsibility of supportin' your family. But at some point, your family would have to find their own support system by utilizing your efforts to grow from. There will come a time when you have to focus on self instead of worrying about everybody else's needs. You have a good heart, Quan, I know this. But there's somethin' in your heart that you really wanna accomplish in life, and that's the goal I'm talking about."

Taquan was quiet for a long moment, and she gave him the patience he needed to think it over.

"Where do you see yourself five years from now?" She finally spoke up to encourage him farther.

"Five years?"

"Yep."

"Other than wit' you," he replied, "a successful gaming software creator. I always wanted to create my own video game. That'll be cool as hell."

"That takes a lot of education, too."

He nodded slowly.

"And a lot of money as well."

Taquan seemed excited about this topic. Da'Jhana noticed.

"Yeah, wit' somethin like that, you have to educate yourself and do a lot of studying," said Taquan.

"And if that don't pan out how you expect it to?"

"You talkin' about a plan B?"

"There should always be a backup plan."

"Um." While Taquan was dwelling on, that his gaze swiveled to the left, outside the large glass window. Something very odd caught his eye, and before he knew it, he was up on his feet, heading towards the exit door.

"Where you going?" Da'Jhana stood up instinctively at the thought of some kind of trouble amiss.

Next door to the McDonalds, across the main entrance parking lot, was a Burger King. It was at the Burger King drive-thru window where Taquan's attention had been attracted.

"Quan, hold up, bae," Da'Jhana called after him as she followed at a fast pace.

Taquan's attention was on the poorly dressed man in the filthy Kangol hat, standing around the drive-thru window, begging people for change as they drove through. The man's name was Red Eddie, and he was a known dopehead in town. This was Lil Eddie's dead-beat father, who he cared about truly, despite his way of life. Last time Red Eddie pulled a move like this, he was high on dope and drunk, and had jumped on some dude who tried to chump him. He got his ass beat and Lil Eddie wanted to murk the dude that did it. Red Eddie still went to jail for it. Taquan was trying to prevent that from happening again. He couldn't let it go down in his presence.

"What're you doing, Red Eddie?" Taquan stepped around a beige Trans-Am to get to the man. Surprisingly, Red Eddie wasn't wasted like he was before.

"Wassup, Quan, my main man? Tryna get my groove on ova here hustlin'," said the dopehead.

"This ain't hustlin', pops. Let's go eat somethin'. I'm ova here at Micky D's wit my girl."

"Dat one right there?" Red Eddie pointed. Taquan glanced back to see Da'Jhana coming up behind him. She then moved around him, took Red Eddie by the sleeve of his South Pole t-shirt and dragged him away from the window.

"That's right, bae," Taquan grinned.

Da'Jhana told Red Eddie that she would stick her foot up his ass, if he didn't behave. Taquan watched and followed close behind. Somehow, Red Eddie knew better than to test her patience. When he entered McDonald's and was led to the booth where the remainder of their food sat, Red Eddie immediately begin stuffing his mouth.

"Slow down, Pops. Dang." Taquan offered him his cup of soda next. "When was the last time you ate somethin', Red Eddie?" he asked.

"One thang I don't do, I don't starve m'self," Red Eddie said with a mouthful of food.

"I can't tell the way you fuckin' that food up." Taquan sat across the table from him with his phone in his hand. He had secretly taken a picture of Red Eddie feeding his face and sent it to Lil Eddie with a short message.

"Y'all heard about the new boyz in town?" Red Eddie had to stop a second to catch a breath.

"What you talkin' bout, Red?"

"Dem new boyz from outta town, ridin' round in the big money trucks and stuff. Yep. Sho' nuff. Just saw' em, not too long ago."

Both Taquan and his girl looked at one another cluelessly.

"How many they was, Pops?"

"Quite a few of 'em, Quan. Drove right by me in that big white money truck."

"What they look like?"

"Damn sho don't look like the Fedz or any of your boyz, or the otherz round here," he said.

It wasn't like Red Eddie to say too much of anything, unless he meant to gain something out of it. He was very resourceful on what's what in the streets.

"Well, I don't know nothin' bout that, Pops."

They sat with Red Eddie for a little while longer, before heading back out for the school. Out front, in the parking lot before the school, Taquan kissed his girl and promised to meet up with her later. "Daj?" he called after her, after she got out and was walking away. "I know what Plan B is."

"Huh?"

He said, "Study for my G.E.D. and go to TCC to get a degree in computer engineering. Then I wanna invest my money in stocks and bonds. You know, can't be a thug all my life."

123

That made her smile. "I like that."

"I love you, bae."

"Love you more." She blew him a kiss. Da'Jhana turned and headed for her next class, not knowing that she would never see him smile again.

Chapter 29

When it happened, Shamar, Bizzy and Chino were conspiring and concocting a plan to deal with a potential threat, who was in the way of them fulfilling a very important task. The buzzing vibration of the cell phone in his right pants pocket demanded his attention. Shamar reached to retrieve the phone, and in doing so, a strange feeling came over him. He didn't dwell on it too much. It was more of a fleeting, absentminded feeling, with no true meaning. But that was until he read the text message from an unfamiliar caller tagged, "Tom Cruise." Shamar didn't know any Tom Cruise, other than the actor, and that was only from his list of action movies.

"Pay up time, sprout. The info and my 20%. Meet at the Four Seasons in downtown NY, 3:00 p.m. Room 201. No exceptions," read Shamar. The text message made his stomach churn.

"That shit sounds suspicious, my nigga," said Bizzy.

"This is LJ's phone I'm using as a backup line. You right, too, brah, it does sound fishy as fuck. Who the hell is Tom Cruise? What information he want from LJ? And 20% payment of what?" Shamar stared down at the phone, like it was some alien object.

"Sound like some creep shit to me," added Chino.

"Most certainly."

"Call him up," Bizzy replied.

Shamar said, "Naw. Let's go meet Tom Cruise ourselves, and see what the play is."

"Now that sounds like a plan." Bizzy rubbed his palms together readily. "To the Four Seasons."

The next sound heard was Chino chambering a round in his Glock 40. This was another recruit from Spanish Harlem area. Chino was a twenty-two-year-old Dominican enforcer, with a solid reputation. The HCG crew now had seventeen new recruits. When Delani gave the order that he wanted more loyal soldiers on their team, Shamar, Bizzy and Shoo Baby went out and scouted some remarkable recruits. It was no easy feat. The seventeen soldiers were carefully selected out of the thirty-something that really had potential.

It also gave Shoo Baby something else to focus on, other than the disappearance of Mookie and Rikah. The explanation was they had decided to part from the team together to go live their lives in harmony elsewhere. They had the money and the brains to have a successful life together, but Shoo Baby wasn't feeling that shit at all. She knew there was something else behind their disappearance, but didn't contest it. It was better to just let sleeping dogs lie. But Shoo Baby wasn't fooled. She knew Shamar and Dejah were keeping the real truth under wraps.

The drive to the Four Seasons was spent planning their attack. The crew wanted answers and there was no other way to get them, except by force and manipulation. When they reached their destination, the trio rode the elevator up to the designated floor. Shamar looked at his watch and saw that it was actually ten minutes till three. Better to be prompt than late.

Four feet from the door of Room 201, that exact door opened and a room service personnel was in the process of retreating with her food cart. But Chino shoved her right back through the door. Both Bizzy and Shamar followed in, with their guns drawn. And sure enough, a Tom Cruise look alike was sitting before a table dish, cutting into a baked potato with a side of medium rare steak. When he looked up at their entry, he was staring down the barrel of Bizzy's chrome .9mm pistol.

"Get the fuck in the corner and put your nose to the wall," Chino told the woman and pushed her in the direction he wanted her to go. Meanwhile, Shamar approached the white man and moved his food settings aside, before snatching up the Wilson Combat 1911 .45 caliber pistol that he had on the nightstand beside him.

"Victor Brewer, FBI? Well, I'll be damned." Shamar had also retrieved the black leather wallet from the nightstand table that contained his official government credentials. He felt betrayed, at that moment, by his own, now deceased, hooligan.

"Strip down," Bizzy said to the FBI agent, with the threat of sending a bullet through his face.

The Tom Cruise look-alike did as he was told. He stripped down to just his boxer briefs.

"This must be some kinda mistake, fellas."

"It's no mistake here, FBI man." Shamar produced the cell phone to show him the text message. "Is this what you sent to this phone?"

The man swallowed nervously. He nodded yes.

"Okay, now what's your business wit' LJ?"

"LJ?" Special Agent Victor Brewer appeared surprised by the name. "I don't know any LJ. He told me his name was Patric, and they called him PK."

"Bullshit," said Chino.

"Straight up bullshit," Bizzy professed. "You're the FBI so how can you not know the muthafucka you g'tting' information from and taxin' them twenty percent, of what? Lie again and I'ma-" Bizzy just went across his head with the pistol anyway to emphasize the threat. "Lie again!"

In the corner, the woman whimpered, like a scared child anticipating getting spanked for being bad. Shamar held up a patient hand.

"Tell me what I need to know," he said to the white FBI agent in the humblest tone.

Brewer nodded softly, as if giving himself permission to reveal what he shouldn't. He didn't want to die and these niggaz looked like they were the real deal. So, he spilled the beans without further hesitation.

The initial person of interest was the brother of a local drug lord by the name of Rashad "Heavy" Simmons, who was his little brother's second-in-command. Heavy Simmons was responsible for many deaths, ranging from New York to Boston, but he seems to always slip away from conviction. One of those deaths was of Aaron Novick, who was another government official investigating an associate of Heavy's and wound up dead in an alley over in Jamaica Queens. A month or so ago, LJ was in the area and proximity of Heavy and assumed to be one of his guys. So, Brewer cornered him one day and squeezed him hard for information that LJ did not have. Unfortunately for LJ, he was forced to infiltrate Heavy's circle to learn what all he could, or else go down along with his whole empire.

"Where the twenty percent come in at?" Bizzy asked.

Shamar had leaned against the wall across from the agent and was watching him very cautiously.

Brewer said, "He looked like a hustler and so I used what I got to get what I need."

"So you're a cooked cop, too?" said Chino.

"I don't think that's all," said Shamar.

The Tom Cruise look-alike saw the menacing glare in his eyes when he looked at him.

Chino pulled out his phone to send out a text he knew would be worthwhile. The agent provided more information that had nothing to do with Hooliganz Crime Gang nor the new system that Delani was running through the surrounding areas. Shamar didn't know whether to be worried or happy his crew wasn't the actual primary targets.

After applying pressure to the agent to get every drop of information from him, Chino stepped over to Shamar to inform him of the final endgame.

"We kill him?" asked Bizzy.

No sooner than he asked the question did a short knock sound at the door.

Chino went to answer it.

"Aren't you married, FBI man?" Shamar asked.

He was married with two sons, and a daughter back in South Adams Basin, New York. He pleaded for the life of his family and Bizzy laughed at him.

Moments later, Chino returned with two young teenage girls, who began shredding their clothes immediately. Then they joined the agent on the bed to perform every style of sexual intercourse with him, while under gunpoint. He could only stand firm for so long before his dick responded, and Chino had it all on video.

"Now you're under my orders," said Shamar.

Total blackmail at its best. Tom Cruise could lose everything, if he didn't cooperate with the terms that were demanded of him.

"Who the hell were the girls?" Bizzy asked, once they were back in traffic.

Chino laughed. "My baby mama's little sister and her homegirl. Extortions a bitch, huh?"

"You already know."

It was part of the game.

Chapter 30

Nakia was the shy, timid one, while Tamia was audacious, conniving and manipulative in every sense. And Toby was in love with them both. There was no doubt in her mind that she would kill for them, if it meant making them smile. She would do anything for them girls. And so would Kordae, who had already proved it. The sacrifices he'd made to assure their safety and that they had something to eat at night was commendable.

Prior to their mother abandoning them for eight days before Toby got involved, they had been living in the dark, with no power in the house, for two weeks straight. It turned out their mother, Shaunie "Fancy" Turner, was a drunk and a heavy cokehead, and had a reputation for setting niggaz up to get jacked, and even killed. Fancy had not been a good mother. She was in jail, facing a rack of felony charges. Apparently, she had found herself way over in Tallahassee one evening, tricking off in some southside trap-house, when the authorities raided the spot. Her and two hustlers were taken in. One of the hustlers implicated her, with a promise to set her up with something nice when they got out, if she went with it.

The dumb bitch indeed went with it. Fancy was already a convicted felon and there would be a long time before she saw the streets again. Fancy never even mentioned her children. She was so high out of her mind when she was arrested that she went with pretty much everything.

"She must knew you was gonna step up and take care of everythang. Ya mama had faith in you," Toby told him.

Kordae just shrugged his bony shoulders.

Toby promised to do what she could. She had admitted to him that she was on the run from the law. Unfortunately, they both were now, and Kordae assured her that he would do his part and not disappoint.

"You just gotta watch out for my sistaz," he said.

"No doubt," Toby hugged him. "You got my word on that."

To keep her word, Toby decided, against her better judgment, to go out and find Faheem "Gangsta" Campbell. This was the twins' father and, due to his neglecting them, Toby wanted to teach him a valuable lesson.

Having become a nightcrawler of late, Toby had familiarized herself with the areas of New Orleans, learning what all she could learn to put things in her own perspective. That came from exhaustively sitting around the house doing nothing, while her wound healed. Her healing process only lasted for so long before the need to explore her new territory became a necessity. She could not sit still for too long.

Toby knew all about who ran the Desire Projectz, she had witnessed the double-homicide that took place outside the Walgreens on Morrison Road one evening. It had been a drug deal gone wrong and Toby knew who the killers were. Just like she knew where to find Gangsta, who lived across the river on the Westbank in Westwego, but hung out consistently on Washington Avenue. It was where his current girlfriend lived, right next to a black owned church. The girlfriend's father was the owner of that very same church. There was a safehouse, where Pastor Vincent Harrel stored drugs inside the church,which was funded by a local drug lord, whose mother Vincent married.

The drug lord's name was Bernard "B-Money" Jones, and Gangsta was one of his many workers, who decided to pursue the Pastor's daughter and won her over. Now Gangsta stayed close to his girlfriend, Tonisha, to keep a close eye on the church, after B-Money appointed him that area to run.

But Gangsta was sloppy, thought Toby, after laying on him for three nights in a row. The nigga was trickin' off with other bitches, one of them was Tonisha's home girl and best friend, right there behind the church. Gangsta was said to be a real deal paymaster. He was obsessed with paying for pussy. It was how he met the twins' mother. He tricked off with Fancy a few times. When Fancy was four months pregnant, she confronted Gangsta, proclaiming that he was the father. He slapped her around and told Fancy just like that, he wasn't taking care of no trick hoe kids. The nerve of this nigga, who had no problem running up in her raw, without considering the consequences. Gangsta was dead wrong.

So, Toby caught him right where she wanted him, in the throes of pleasure, getting his dicked sucked behind the church in a parked car. His head was leaning back against the driver seat headrest, while he gripped the back of the head of the bitch givin' him oral service.

"You's a stupid ass nigga," muttered Toby. Then she drew her gun and sent five slugs into Gangsta's face and torso, killing him dead. Then she vanished from the scene. The next day, her and Kordae were sitting in the living room watching the Channel 13 News. The news capture was of Gangsts's murder and the incident believed to be related to another incident recently of a murdered street hustler.

Kordae leaned his head against Toby's shoulder and said, "Your secret is safe wit' me, Toby." Without saying a word, Toby leaned over and kissed the top of his head.

What was understood didn't need to be explained.

They were a family now.

Family sticks together.

Toby was in the bathroom two days later, staring at her reflection in the mirror over the sink. Her face was expressionless as she stared at the scars upon it. She had been

LAND OF THE HOOLIGANZ 4 | IRA B

stabbed in the face twice, one taking one of her eyes and the other upon her right cheek. Her wounds were not yet fully healed, especially the ones along her chest, arms and stomach. But the scars meant nothing to her. She had multiple other battle wounds to mark her journey. Toby was a warrior.

Prior to meeting Delani and becoming his sidekick, Toby was affiliated with the Billy's Blood Gang, an organization from which her real reputation started. Being one of the few female Bloods in her area, Toby had to go extra hard to earn her keep in the sect.

There was no place she felt she could go where her respect wouldn't be acknowledged. One could look at her and automatically know she was official. But today, she was about to make her presence known. The gangsta in her couldn't just sit around and watch the world revolve around her, without being active in it. As she donned on her Prada sunglasses and checked her new haircut, (Toby had decided to chop away her long hair for an Amber Rose cut) she nodded to herself and exited the bathroom.

Thanks to Debra, she had provided her with her own wheels to get around in. Now Toby was able to go wherever she wanted in her new Lexus SUV. And today she was taking her new family out to eat. This would be her first time ever going out during the daytime. It was time for a change, and by all means, she would take advantage of it.

Chapter 31

Before Monique could react in time, the palm impacting against her face with a vicious slap almost sent her sprawling to the floor in the process.

"Get the hell outta my damn house," Tabitha snarled over at Monique, like an angry hyena.

Monique righted herself and glared at the other woman.

"You heard what she said," said Donnie Walker, who was Tabitha's cousin Nashondras's husband. Prior to Monique stopping by the house, Donnie was already there, out back mowing the grass. He had come in just in time to witness Tabitha verbally insinuating that Monique had something to do with Thump's murder. With her hands clenched, as if she was deciding whether to hit her best friend's mother back or not, Monique watched as the big man stepped in between them.

"Don't make me force you out, little girl."

"Don't touch me," Monique hissed at him, then shot Tabitha a menacing look over his shoulder. "You can believe what you wanna believe, Mama Tee, but I know I had nothin' to do wit' any of that shit. Vee and Thump were family to me." she said with conviction

"And it won't be the first time family turn on their own," retorted Tabitha. "Get her outta my face, Donnie."

Needing no further encouragement, Donnie began shoving Monique towards the front door. She resisted against his roughness, but her one hundred forty-five pounds was no match against his two hundred sixty pound frame. He all but tossed her out on her ass onto the grass outside the front door. Tabitha had followed the procession all the way out to the front porch.

"And the next time you step foot on my property, I'ma put a bullet in that ass, you bitch," she spat venom.

Monique ignored her as she marched for the car. It was black with chrome trimming G-Wagon that Heaven had bought her for her nineteenth birthday. She didn't even look back as she got back behind the wheel of her vehicle and drove away with tears welling in her eyes.

Anger burned in her chest.

If it had been anybody else, they would have gotten hands put on them for slapping her.

What Monique didn't understand was what brought this on, for Tabitha to turn on her like that. That made Monique reflect back on the day of Veronica and Thump's funeral. During the services, Monique had conversed with Tabitha, gave her sincerest condolences and had even sat next to the woman throughout the whole ceremony. From the church to the burial site and back to Lake Skillet, where the cookout block party ceremony took place, Monique had been there every step of the way.

After that day, Tabitha had gone into seclusion to mourn her losses alone, without everybody worrying over her. Monique had pretty much done the same, but it was Heaven, who had kept her on her toes. Heaven told her that she had to respect Tabitha's mind and honor the space she desired.

Today was the second attempt in trying to visit Tabitha, after not seeing her for well over a month. At first, she had been ecstatic to be near her best friend's mother again, after so long of an absence. Just like she had done many other times before, Monique saw the front door open and let herself through the screen door. Little did she know what lay beyond.

That was when her tears came, and Monique cried quietly as she rode through traffic. She wasn't sure whether she should be angry with herself or Tabitha for what she did. All she knew was that she wanted to release her wrath on something. Since it couldn't be Tabitha, she needed a stress reliever. She needed a blunt.

No sooner than the thought crossed her mind did she wipe her eyes with the back of her hand and look up to see the BP gas station coming up ahead. They called this spot two o'clock, since that was the time it closed at night. The BP was just up the street from the New Projectz, which was where Monique currently lived in her own apartment.

Upon turning into the side entrance of the Two o'clock, she also spotted parked out front was Lil One's candy painted Infiniti truck and Roz's royal blue Lamborghini truck. There was a total of five HCG member posted up outside the station politicking, two niggas and three women. When Monique pulled up on the scene, all their eyes swiveled in her direction as she yoked the G-Wagon to a screeching halt, inches behind the Lambo truck.

"What it do, lil sis?" Greeted Roz, who was accompanied by Tootsie and her girl Whitney. Roz was one of the oldest females in the crew, thirty years old, and whose reputation for puttin' in work was without blemish.

"Yall check this out," Monique replied and beckoned them to follow her.

Tootsie and Lil One looked at one another, shrugged their shoulders, and followed behind Monique, who led them all around back of the two o'clock. The group of drunks and dopeheads, who were known to occupy the area alongside the building, scattered. All it took was one look at Monique and her entourage and they understood that they needed to get the fuck from 'round there.

"What's going on, Mo?" asked Mane, seeing as she was removing all her jewelry and pocketing it.

"I'm trying to get down wit' the crew."

"What?" Lil One reacted.

"You heard me," snapped Monique.

"Nah, lil sis, it ain't going down like that. That's not our call," said Roz

"So, it's Hev's call? Fuck that. I'm ready."

Tootsie said, "This not your thang, Mo. Don't you get it? There's a valid reason why you ain't Hooliganz Crime Gang, and we're not about to breach that protocol."

"Suit yourselves," said Monique. Then the first punch landed solidly to Roz's jaw before Monique spun on Mane and hit him with a fast two-piece. When Lil One stepped forward to restrain her, Monique side-stepped him with an overhand right to his right eye.

By this time, Roz was already springing forward and hitting Monique with a hard left hook to the jaw.

"Yeah. That's what I'm talkin' bout." Monique counter-attacked and went for what she knew.

The rest of the hooliganz tossed caution aside and pounced on her ass, like a tic on a dog.

Monique gave them hell for a little petite bitch, surprising the crew when she refused to back down. The pressure was on. But the showdown didn't last long before a gunshot blast rang out and everybody stopped what they were doing. They stared down at themselves and at one another to see who had the audacity to produce a weapon.

"The fuck y'all think y'all doing back here?"

All eyes turned in the direction of the voice and saw Vonte standing a few feet away clutching his Glock .23. When Vonte laid eyes on Monique, he frowned and tucked his pistol back at his waist.

"Really? Y'all got a death wish or somethin?" Vonte asked as he approached Monique.

"It's all good," Monique shrugged. "It was my call, Von."

"Your call for what?"

No one responded except for Monique.

"I'm HCG now. Since they wouldn't give it to me, I decided to take it instead."

All Vonte could do was shake his head wearily. "And you think Hev is going to agree to this shit?"

"She will have no choice."

"She won't?" Vonte questioned.

"I'll deal wit' my sista myself." Monique turned to Roz and extended her hand.

Reluctantly, Roz smirked through bloody teeth, took her hand and embraced her. "Welcome to Hooliganz Crime Gang, lil sis."

In turn, Mane stepped forward to show Monique some love, then Lil One, Tootsie and Whitney. When it was Vonte's turn, he hesitated. Everybody looked at him expectantly, seeing the disdain in his eyes.

"What's done can't be undone," sighed Vonte. He opened out his arms and Monique stepped into them.

"Welcome to the crew, Mo," he said. "Welcome home."

Chapter 32

The hollow-point slug spiraled its way up the barrel, through the silencer, and drilled its way through Bre's forehead, destroying everything in its path toward the back of her skill and taking with it chunks of bone, brain and flesh. The momentum of the impact propelled Bre, slamming against the back of the metal-folding chair and tilting it backwards on both rear legs before crashing into the floor. Rachet glanced over at Junior and saw that there was no emotion on his face.

A couple feet away from her dead friend sat Lele, who too was bound and filled with helplessness. When she saw Junior turn to her next, with that murderous look in his eyes, she knew her time had come. For the past two and a half days of being tortured for information, Lele begged for a quick death. She didn't even blink or cringe in fear when the gun was pressed into the middle of her forehead.

Lele gritted what was left of her shattered teeth and pushed her head against the tip of the silencer. She was so ready for it to be done and over with.

"She's eager to die now," Stank announced from where he stood nearby watching.

Junior looked into her blacken swollen-shut eyes as she peered back at him through slits. Lele's whole head was two times bigger than its normal size. If she did not die from a bullet, she would have eventually bit the dust due to internal head injury.

"I hope you go right where Uncle Pitt and Dyamond at so y'all can resettle your differences there," Junior stated a second before squeezing the trigger.

Minutes later, jugs of gasoline were being doused all throughout the old abandoned house, way out in the country of Havana, off of Highway 27. Both Rachet and Stank made sure the bodies were well drenched before they set fire to the place.

A little while after that, Junior and his crew were back on the road again. But this time, they were headed out of Tallahassee, where the team had been staying for the past two weeks. Earlier on, Junior just wanted to declare war against the HCG crew, but he had to exercise patience gain the advantage. After calling up more enforcers to assist him with his plan of attack, Junior saw to it that they learned the areas first. He had twenty-three of his Money Steppaz Gang members present and spread out throughout the two counties. After torturing all the information out of Lele and Bre, regarding their crew and security, such information with advanced infiltration, the MSG clique were ready to wreak havoc, like never before.

Junior was about to give HCG a taste of their own medicine. What he had planned for them would no doubt make history in the two neighboring counties. Hooliganz Crime Gang were about to meet their match. Junior would soon be King.

The information provided was enough to cripple HCG's whole operation. Bre had been very vocal when under extreme pressure. Compounding that with what Junior already knew from HCG's reputation, he could actually say that the notorious street gang wasn't all that untouchable.

They could be dismantled.

Destroyed even.

Who Junior really wanted was Shamar. He would give anything to come face to face with his old foe again. He would just have to wait his turn. When that opportunity presented itself, Shamar was gonna wish he never crossed him. A wicked smirk appeared on Junior's face at the thought of being the element of surprise that was about to give the Hooliganz Crime Gang a run for the money. Money Steppaz Gang was taking over.

Once they made it to Tallahassee, where his presence was anticipated, Junior and his crew got out onto the premises of Joe Lewis Apartments. This was one of the territories HCG did not claim. Roe Collins and his Gangsta Disciples were the rulers of this land. The whole Northside was run by the GDs, and unfortunately they had a mutual respect for one another. The GDs and HCG were business associates, but when it came down to personal matters outside of business, both parties kept their distance from each other.

"Everythang copacetic, my G?" said Roe when Junior entered his apartment building to see that the older gangsta was cradling his infant son.

Junior took a seat across from Roe, who used to go with his mother back in the day. Junior remembered home from growing up and Roe always stopping by to make sure the family was straight. Junior remembered when Roe took out the time to drop jewels of wisdom on him, when he was just a youngsta. Roe was one of the few niggas that he still had respect for back home, having never given him reason to doubt his position.

"It's all good, Roe. It won't be long now, and I'll be outta your hair," Junior said.

"You're always welcomed on this side," ensured Roe as he stood up to deposit his son into the baby crib across the room, where he could sleep in peace.

What Roe didn't know was that Junior had a whole squad of Steppaz out there waiting for the call to attack and demolish Hooliganz Crime Gang. He only knew of the crew he came up with. Roe, to his understanding, was under the impression that Junior had come back to visit family, and sow some seeds, where his hustle game was concerned. But

Roe wasn't one to be told just anything, he knew Junior was on a murder mission. He'd had some of his guys to trail Junior, and his crew and reported back to him what they learned.

"Going against HCG is a bold move," Roe stated with his back turned to him. Junior stiffened and stared up at the man standing before him.

"Who said anything about that, my G?"

"Your actions."

"My actions?" frowned Junior.

"It's none of my business, Junior, but I hope you know what you're doing. Hooliganz Crime Gang is deadly. They're smart and very cautious, to a fault. But overall, they are militant and flawless at warfare."

Junior did not respond.

"Latrice know?" asked Roe

"No," Junior said slowly. If his mother knew what he was up to, she would have a fit. It was bad enough that she had to accept the fact that he was out there thuggin' in the streets.

Roe shook his head and turned to face him. "The only reason why I'm doing this is outta love and respect for your mama, and of course, you, Junior."

"Doing what?"

"Let's take a walk outside." Roe beckoned him as he headed for the door.

With a deep sigh, Junior rose to his feet and followed Roe out the door. "What about your lil man?"

"He's protected, my G."

"Your trust grows deep for you guys."

"It's a necessity." Roe greeted some of his GD soldiers upon his exit outside in the night. In passing, he dapped up his people, and dept it moving.

Junior followed, in the process acknowledging his steppaz, who also stood amongst the others.

Four buildings down, Roe led the way into another apartment, where two sentries guarded the door with semiautomatic weapons. Inside, a total of two more of the guys greeted them as Roe continually led the way to a rear bedroom in the apartment.

"Damn," was all Junior could say when he entered the room, which contained an arsenal of weapons of various calibers and sizes. Roe approached what appeared to be a deep freezer and opened the lid to reveal an arsenal of guns inside. The room even smelled like gun powder, steel and the unmistakable scent of cold hard maliciousness.

"To take down an army, like HCG, you'll need the proper equipment," said Roe.

Junior's eyes caught something that attracted him directly towards it. He walked over and removed it from the gun shelf on the far back wall. "What's this one?"

"That's McMillan TAc-50 right there, my G, a fifty seven-inch rifle that shoots .50 caliber Browning machine gun rounds. You can hit your target from a mile away wit' that muthafucker there."

"I want it," Junior said, glancing over at him.

Roe smiled. "It's all yours."

But he didn't stop there, Junior summoned for his steppaz to come have their picks. It was about to go down in the streets.

Chapter 33

Four days after the incident with Monique at the two o'clock, Heaven received the call she had been both dreading and anxiously anticipating. For days, the search for Lele and Bre had proceeded. Day after day, night after night, the hooliganz and some loyal others roamed through nearby towns, slithering through dark alley and around abandoned buildings, any place where they could be possibly found.

Undeterred, Heaven and Jamir kept on their mission to find them, even paying someone to go into the jailhouse to see if they were there, as well. Neither were anywhere to be found, and that notion put the whole team on edge. Heaven was in the process of securing a business proposition with a leasing agent, about a building where she wanted to start her cafe lounge. Lately, the team had been buying up all available building spaces to fill them with potential businesses, all around the town. By doing this, they were offering more job opportunities for the people. They were backed and insured by some very credible associates, who were receiving their pieces of the pie as well. Hooliganz Crime Gang was doing some major things before the suspicious disappearance of two of her own.

"What is it?" demanded Heaven, having to step aside, out of earshot, to take the call.

"Got some bad new, sis."

She closed her eyes. "I'm listening."

It was Kweli who had called to deliver the news. "It's happened again, Hev."

"What happened?"

"There's a total of thirteen more of our own who disappeared overnight," he said.

"Thirteen?" she gasped. The real estate agent looked up from his computer behind the dark wooded desk. Across from him was Eugenia Wakefield, a friend of Heaven, who she met in college, and who was studying real estate contract and business.

When Kweli ran down the list of names of those who were missing, she felt her heart drop. Panic was somewhere close, and Heaven could feel it trying to sneak its way in. Apparently, over the course of the night, thirteen hooliganz had been snatched up, kidnapped or simply vanished into thin air, without anyone being the wiser. But Heaven just couldn't go for that, somebody had to have witnessed something. Thirteen people were just too many for someone not to have seen something go down.

"Listen to me, Kweli. Round up the whole team and have everybody meet me in thirty at the spot.

"Say no more, Sis?"

"Kweli?"

"Yeah."

"Make sure you have Detective Lady present, too, because her services will also be needed," said Heaven, referring to Detective Angie Galloway. She hung up with Kweli and the urge to release a viscous lioness roar, indicating her frustration, was very tempting.

Her business awaited her.

"Um Eugenia?" Heaven approached the pair and came to stand next to her friend. "Would it be too much to ask for you to continue without my presence? You already know my plans and budget. There's been a family emergency, and my presence is needed."

"Of course, Heaven. I'll finish up the paperwork here and forward everything to you later," said Eugenia.

"You are the best, girl."

"Likewise."

Heaven kissed her cheek and headed straight for the exit doors, where her security lied. Upon her exit, three well-armed hooliganz escorted her to her vehicle. She got into the backseat of the bulletproof Mercedes Benz truck, with one of her hooliganz claiming the seat next to her.

"I take it you heard the news?" said Lolita Shaw, the one behind the wheel.

Heaven ignored her and proceeded to call Debra on speed dial, and stopped. The Italian mobstress had done her part by securing Heaven her caliber of power and the proper tools she needed to strengthen her empire and make a fortune from it. Debra decided to remain in the shadows now that her job was done. She was only needed to be called when things got too detrimental. It was a final resort to contact her. Until then, Heaven had the power and brains to control whatever pressures came her way, and utilize it to capitalize from. There was no need to call Debra.

"I got this," Heaven told herself before looking up front and announcing where she wanted to go.

"Already know," Lolita said.

Heaven called Jamir, who in turned linked in Tilly on a merged call. By this time, her team was definitely in panic-mode.

"What can you tell me, Jay?" Heaven asked as an incoming call from Taquan came through. Just recently, he had lost his grandma, Bertha Mae, who suddenly died in her sleep, and he'd been torn over it since. It was Da'Jhana who was there to keep him together. She ignored Taquan's call.

"I got some people out here investigating right now. So far, there's been no sign of foul play involved."

"What's the number in total?"

"Thirteen," said Tilly.

"And Marco was one of those thirteen," a somber Jamir said. "He also just recently earned a major record deal with rapper Future's label, and was set to head out to Atlanta this weekend to finalize the music contract."

"There's no doubt some foul play involved in this whole situation," commented Heaven.

"I agree. Any idea who could be behind this shit? I mean, this has to be an act of some type of warfare tactic or somethin'," said Tilly.

"To take thirteen of our own in one night, without makin' any noise? That's some secret military, Navy Seal type shit goin' on round here," Jamir said.

"It's something." Heaven was thinking and wondering if Bully Gang was behind this situation. They too were of a militant nature, but Bully Gang was one of HCG's biggest investors. Pl,us Heaven had a few of her people working undercover within the Bully Gang's inner circle who would have pulled the plug on it first. Well at least that's what she hoped, but truthfully, Heaven didn't see Bully Gang pulling a stunt like this.

This was something else entirely.

"What about the Feds-" Jamir's words were cut short by a weird thumping sound. Then almost a second later, the blare of a car horn sounded off, just before the terrifying sound of metal colliding against metal in what was not to be mistaken for a car crash.

That was when Heaven's heart dropped.

"Jay," she screamed.

Chapter 34

White Boy Ty and Shamoorah had just gotten into the condo from the Children's Hospital on Phillipps Road, where Nikita had a scheduled doctor's appointment with the cardiac specialist. Baby girl was born with a heart murmur, and the procedure today was the first of many more to come during the course of her existence.

While they were gone, Abigail was holding the fort down, but she was not alone, for Zamon had found his way into her life and Abigail was smitten. However, Ty made it clear that if Zamon was going to continue to pursue Abigail, while still being active in the streets, they would have to take their business elsewhere. The last thing Ty needed was for Zamon to bring trouble to his doorstep and jeopardize the wellbeing of his family. To White Boys Ty's surprise, Zamon had really been on some chill, calm, cool and collected shit. With the new statuses in the crew, Zamon had been maintaining his business side of things. With Abigail's help, he'd upstarted his own nail shop and food truck, and had even invested in some stocks and bonds. Ever since meeting Abigail, everything had been going right for him, and he was not about to mess that up. Ty was proud of him, too. It was time for growth.

As far as Ty was concerned, the streets were of little importance to him now. Raising his daughter and being a constant participant in her life was priority. But don't get it twisted, he was still that certified gangsta, just a sense of true purpose defined his current position White Boy Ty just wanted to be there for Nikita.

He still had dreams of Toby killing him one day, but Ty knew that would never happen. Although he had yet to speak to her, Ty knew by faith that she was making due with her situation. Toby was no fool, she was determined to win. By any means necessary, she would fulfill her heart's desires. Toby and Ty would always have one another in faith and through unshakable love.

"What y'all got going on up in here?" Shamoorah acknowledged Abigail and Zamon.

"Zee!" Nikita ran up to Zamon on wobbly, chubby legs and demanded to be picked up.

Abigail stroked the child's curly hair and said, "We just got back from seeing Zee's mama and takin' her out to lunch."

"Oh yeah?" Ty shot his boy a curious glance. "She gets to meet the mama now, brah?"

Zamon grinned as he tickled Nikita's ribs and sent her shrieking with glee.

"And pretty much neglected me the whole time. I damn near had to threaten they asses to get some attention," he said. "But it's all love-" Zamon paused when his cellphone rang, interrupting his vibe.

"Hullo! Hullo!" Nikita bellowed at the sound of the phone ringing, and put an imaginary phone to her ear. When Zamon checked the caller ID and saw that it was Lil Eddie calling, something suddenly came over him. Baby girl sensed his dismay, and then climbed over onto Abigail's lap next.

Right then, White Boy Ty's phone rang, and he fished in his pants pocket to get it. Shamoorah didn't know what it was exactly, but she did not feel right, all of a sudden. A premonition washed over her as she looked over at her man.

"What's up, B?" Ty answered.

"Jamir is dead," cried Baiyina.

Ty instantly felt his heart squeeze with fear. "Dead?" Ty said, and glanced blankly over at Zamon, who too was on the phone with a troubled look on his face. "What do you mean Jamir is dead? How?" he snapped, startling his baby girl.

"Somebody…" Baiyina was trying to keep it together. "He was caught slippin' in traffic. Somebody shot him, Ty. They killed Jamir," she cried.

Before Ty even realized what he was doing, he flung the phone across the room. It shattered upon impact, when it met the wall next to the electric fireplace. His actions really scared Nikita, and she began to cry and call out for her mother. But White Boy Ty was already headed straight for the door with that look in his eyes.

Shammorah darted over to the door to block his way. He glared at her. She glared back.

"Move," he hissed at her. "I need to go. My crew need me right now," Ty replied grimly.

"No," Shamoorah stood firmly. "We need you. Your daughter needs you right now," she said.

"Please don't make me move you myself, Moorah. Don't make me do it in font of baby girl," he said.

"And I'll break your fuckin' hands, too," she challenged him, just as Nikita ran up to her. She knelt down to scoop her up. Her gaze never left Ty's, and he looked like he wanted to test her.

"Brah?" Zamon called out to him, and White Boy Ty turned at his voice.

Abigail was up on her feet now. Zamon gave her an apologetic look that she didn't want to see.

"It's bad, my nigga." Zamon then told him about Marco, and how him and the others were taken overnight without anyone knowing. "Then they just hit Jay, Bred Man, Riri, Baby Gangsta, Sheena, and Olo. They all dead, brah. Somebody just initiated war against us."

"Did they say who?

"Nobody has a clue, my nigga!"

"What about Hev? What's her status?"

Zamon told him about the emergency meeting the team was having at their new location. The location was the old V-12 Club building out in the St. Hebron area. It was one of the crew's latest developments, which they were planning to turn into a strip club.

"You two need to stay put until further notice," suggested Shamoorah. "HCG has more than enough soldiers to regroup properly and figure out a way to accomplish the task they're faced with."

Ty looked at Shamoorah for a long moment, then turned away from her and marched right by Zamon for his room. He was not in his right state of mind.

"Take her," Shamoorah handed Abigail her daughter and Nikita fussed about it.

Zamon said, "This shit is fucked up."

"And you better not leave this condo either, Zee. Don't play with me, boy!" Shamoorah then hurried after White Boy Ty to see what was going on with him. Shit was about to go down. It was war.

In the bedroom, Ty was standing in the doorway of the big walk-in closet. He had peeled off his Gucci t-shirt already and was pulling over a gray bullet proof vest. The rippled muscles in his back pronounced that Ty was in awesome shape and far from soft bodied. This white boy was pure gangsta, and Lord only knows what was going through his mind at that moment.

"I know you know how much this means to me." Ty turned to face her. He was hurting and it shone in his eyes. White Boy Ty wanted to cry so badly, but he was forcing himself to hold it in.

"I know," she sighed.

"I promise to be careful, Moorah."

"There's no carefulness in war, Ty. You can't promise me that. Death is a certainty and there's no guarantee that you'll make it out alive.

"You just gotta have faith," he said.

"Fuck faith!" Shamoorah threw her arms around his neck and cried upon his bullet proofed chest. "I love you, nigga. Can't you see that?"

Chapter 35

With the shake of his head, Junior was astounded by how easy Hooliganz Crime Gang was making it for him and his team. All they had to do was lie in wait and let them come to them. And that's exactly what they did, all seventy-one of them, having pulled up in droves of vehicles.

When he was laying on the crew those two weeks, he had suspected the old club was HCG's headquarters. But when he learned from Bre and Lele that it was indeed, he automatically knew what their next move would be. They led one another into their own trap.

Literally.

Heaven figured meeting in town at their usual spot up on the Black would be too wide open and familiar to whomever the unknown enemy was. Little did she know, her own hooliganz had already shown her hand. That's why Junior had done what he did by snatching up some of them to create panic. Then he released fire upon them through a hail of bullets, a cause for an emergency meeting with the whole team. To get ahead, Junior had to think like them, put himself in their shoes and see things in a different angle.

If he didn't know any better, Junior would probably have done the same exact thing. But he knew better. He knew they needed to put their heads together to strategize a master plan. He knew his next move was his best move.

Almost checkmate time.

LAND OF THE HOOLIGANZ 4 | IRA B

"Everybody in position?" Junior said into the thin microphone that hung in front of his square jaw. After a brief second, a confirmation came crackling through his earpiece from the eight shooters he had positioned around the big building, out of sight.

There were six armed hooliganz guarding the front, back and side door entrance of the club. They wore mean mugs on their faces, strapped with heavy artillery, ready to pop off at the slightest hint of a threat.

"Press play," Junior spoke in a precise voice.

Simultaneously, all eight snipers targeted in on the six hooliganz and laid them down, all at once, from their military grade silenced weapons.

"Next up," said Junior.

Out of nowhere rushed another team of ten, as they approached the club's three entrances. Up ahead, there were another three steppaz on top of the building. In their grasp, they carried red metal gas cans, which they began pouring down into the building's input ventilation systems.

Meanwhile, gasoline was being dashed all over the outside entrance doors.

Then came the three cars, which the steppaz had driven up, pressing the frames against each door to prevent anyone from escaping the fury that was about to befall them. When that was completed, Junior gave the order to light that muthafucker up. And lit it up they did.

The whole club seemed to have engulfed in flames almost immediately. Then came the panicked screams from inside the club. It was pure horror. To know that you were trapped inside a burning furnace with no chance of escape. But the steppaz repositioned themselves around the big club, just in case.

The petrifying sounds that reverberated from inside the club were nightmarish. It was so surreal, like they were actually burning in hell. It was the scariest thing to ever experience. Junior grinned like it was music to his ears, especially when a deafening explosion from inside the building erupted. He had no doubt in his mind that this would go down in history.

The Hooliganz Crime Gang was no more.

It was over.

And now there was a new ruler in town.

Epilogue

Two years later.

After destroying the empire of Hooliganz Crew Gang a little over a year ago, Junior reclassified himself back in Quincy and made it his home again. During the beginning stages of his new position of power, he'd survived scandal after scandal and hung on to his role, like a vicious Pitbull.

Junior had been pulled into the abyss of street politics, and like so many rulers before him, he'd checked his conscience and morals at the door. For Junior, such things as integrity, hard work, taking charge of one's life and individual freedom had little meaning. To him, being the King of the streets was still not enough. It was about him holding on to power, no matter what he had to go through to keep it.

Junior was addicted to power, no different than a dopehead was addicted to crack. He always needed more, and he could never get enough, which has been many people's downfall. Wanting too much of what you already have is bad for you.

It's being greedy.

And greed was always the breaking point.

The Bentley Continental turned off of Crawfordville Highway and wound its way through the residential streets of Woodville. Three blocks before its destination, the Bentley passed a dar colored SUV. Inside were three armed goons, who had been waiting, waiting and preparing for this very moment for so long.

Junior though he was slick by moving almost an hour away from where he ruled the streets of Quincy. He was very adequate at the habit of not being followed. But through his power struck blindness, all it took was for one simple mishap to change the game for him.

The Bentley stopped in front of Junior's $1.4 million dollar brownstone, and he allowed his driver to get out and open the door for him. He got out, and up the steps he went to his front door. He then entered the security code to gain entrance to his home. When the door opened and Junior stepped into the foyer, he sighed with relief and shut the door behind him. He was dead tired. Junior kicked off his fifteen hundred dollar loafers right there in the foyer. He tossed his keys down on a table to the right of the door and reached to switch on the light.

What he saw next made his eyes bulge. Then he reached for the gun in his shoulder holster. That very same instant, he was yanked off his feet and slammed face first into the marble floor.

"Lemme get that, bitch nigga," said White Boy Ty as he relieved Junior of the gun. Then he looked up into the face of none other than Toby herself.

"We're about to have fun wit' this fool," said Delani, with a devilish grin on his face.

"Lemme get first dibs, though," Shamar said, before he squatted down next to Junior's head. "Hey homebody. You remember me?" he sneered.

Junior was so scared he was speechless.

He knew he was doomed.

Hooliganz Crime Gang was back.

The End.

Lock Down Publications and Ca$h Presents
Assisted Publishing Packages

Due to an increase in the price of services we have increased our prices. The prices below reflect the price increase as of 11/1/24.

BASIC PACKAGE	UPGRADED PACKAGE
$699	$1000
Editing	Typing
Cover Design	Editing
Formatting	Cover Design
	Formatting
	Upload eBooks to Amazon
	Upload Paperback to Amazon
ADVANCE PACKAGE	**LDP SUPREME PACKAGE**
$1,400	$1,700
Typing	Typing
Editing (line editing/content)	Editing (line editing/content)
Cover Design	Cover Design
Formatting	Formatting
Copyright Registration	Copyright Registration
Proofreading	Proofreading
Upload eBooks to Amazon	Set up Amazon Account
Upload Paperback to Amazon	Upload eBooks to Amazon
	Upload Paperback to Amazon
	Advertise on LDP's Amazon and Facebook Page

***
Other services available upon request.
Additional charges may apply

Lock Down Publications
P.O. Box 944
Stockbridge, GA 30281-9998
Phone: 470 303-9761
Email: lockdownpublications@gmail.com

158

Submission Guideline

Submit the first three chapters of your completed manuscript to ldpsubmissions@gmail.com. In the subject line add **Your Book's Title**. The manuscript must be in a Word Doc file and sent as an attachment. Document should be in Times New Roman, double spaced, and in size 12 font. Also, provide your synopsis and full contact information. If sending multiple submissions, they must each be in a separate email.

Have a story but no way to send it electronically? You can still submit to LDP/Ca$h Presents. Send in the first three chapters, written or typed, of your completed manuscript to:

LDP: Submissions Dept
P.O. Box 944
Stockbridge, GA 30281-9998

DO NOT send original manuscript. Must be a duplicate. Provide your synopsis and a cover letter containing your full contact information.

Thanks for considering LDP and Ca$h Presents.

NEW RELEASES

BLOODLINE OF A SAVAGE 1-3
THESE VICIOUS STREETS 1-3
RELENTLESS GOON 1-3
BY PRINCE A. TAUHID

THE BUTTERFLY MAFIA 1-3
BY FUMIYA PAYNE

A THUG'S STREET PRINCESS 1&2
BY MEESHA

CITY OF SMOKE 3
BY MOLOTTI

GET IT IN SLUGS 1 &2
BY B. STALL

STANDING ON HER BUSINESS 1&2
BY DG SANTANA

STEPPERS 1,2&3
THE REAL BADDIES OF CHI-RAQ
BY KING RIO

THE LANE 1&2
BY KEN-KEN SPENCE

THUG OF SPADES 1&2
LOVE IN THE TRENCHES 2
CORNER BOYS
BY COREY ROBINSON

TIL DEATH 3
BY ARYANNA

THE BIRTH OF A GANGSTER 4
BY DELMONT PLAYER

PRODUCT OF THE STREETS 1-3
BY DEMOND "MONEY" ANDERSON

NO TIME FOR ERROR
BY KEESE

MONEY HUNGRY DEMONS 1-2
BY TRANAY ADAMS

HUB CITY MENACE 1-3
BY J. WHITE

A THUGGISH PASSION 1&2
LAND OF DA HOOLIGANZ 1-4
KILLAZ ON STANDBY 1&2
BY IRA B.

FO'EVA ROLLIN 1&2
BY ASSA RAYMOND BAKER

THE LEVEL UP 1&3
BY LUXURY KING

Coming Soon from Lock Down Publications/Ca$h Presents

IF YOU CROSS ME ONCE 6
ANGEL V
By Anthony Fields

A THUGS STREET PRINCESS 3
By Meesha

CORNER BOYS 2
By Corey Robinson

THA TAKEOVER
By Keith Chandler

BETRAYAL OF A G 2
By Ray Vinci

SAVAGE FAMILY EMPIRE 1&2
SOULLESS GOON 1,2&3
THE DIRTY SIDE OF MONEY 1,2&3
By Prince

FOR MY ENEMY'S SAKE
AMBITIONS OF A SLIDER
FRESH OFF DA PORCH
By IRA B.

THE TRUCKLOAD 1-4
TIPPIN' THE SCALES 1-3
BAD BITCHES WIT GUNZ 3
PROBLEM SOLVED 2
By Christopher "Diesel" Hornezes

Available Now

RESTRAINING ORDER 1 & 2
By **CA$H & Coffee**

LOVE KNOWS NO BOUNDARIES 1-3
By **Coffee**

RAISED AS A GOON I, II, III & IV
BRED BY THE SLUMS I, II, III
BLAST FOR ME I & II
ROTTEN TO THE CORE I II III
A BRONX TALE I, II, III
DUFFLE BAG CARTEL I II III IV V VI
HEARTLESS GOON I II III IV V
A SAVAGE DOPEBOY I II
DRUG LORDS I II III
CUTTHROAT MAFIA I II
KING OF THE TRENCHES
By **Ghost**

LAY IT DOWN I & II
LAST OF A DYING BREED I II
BLOOD STAINS OF A SHOTTA I & II III
By **Jamaica**

LOYAL TO THE GAME I II III
LIFE OF SIN I, II III
By **TJ & Jelissa**

IF LOVING HIM IS WRONG…I & II
LOVE ME EVEN WHEN IT HURTS I II III
By **Jelissa**

PUSH IT TO THE LIMIT
By **Bre' Hayes**

LAND OF THE HOOLIGANZ 4 | IRA B

BLOODY COMMAS I & II
SKI MASK CARTEL I, II & III
KING OF NEW YORK I II, III IV V
RISE TO POWER I II III
COKE KINGS I II III IV V
BORN HEARTLESS I II III IV
KING OF THE TRAP I II
By **T.J. Edwards**

WHEN THE STREETS CLAP BACK I & II III
THE HEART OF A SAVAGE I II III IV
MONEY MAFIA I II
LOYAL TO THE SOIL I II III
By **Jibril Williams**

A DISTINGUISHED THUG STOLE MY HEART I II & III
LOVE SHOULDN'T HURT I II III IV
RENEGADE BOYS 1-4
PAID IN KARMA 1-3
SAVAGE STORMS 1-3
AN UNFORESEEN LOVE 1-3
BABY, I'M WINTERTIME COLD 1-3
A THUG'S STREET PRINCESS 1&2
By **Meesha**

A GANGSTER'S CODE 1-3
A GANGSTER'S SYN 1-3
THE SAVAGE LIFE 1-3
CHAINED TO THE STREETS 1-3
BLOOD ON THE MONEY 1-3
A GANGSTA'S PAIN 1-3
BEAUTIFUL LIES AND UGLY TRUTHS
CHURCH IN THESE STREETS
By **J-Blunt**

CUM FOR ME 1-8
An LDP Erotica Collaboration

BLOOD OF A BOSS 1-5
SHADOWS OF THE GAME
TRAP BASTARD
By **Askari**

THE STREETS BLEED MURDER 1-3
THE HEART OF A GANGSTA 1-3
By **Jerry Jackson**

WHEN A GOOD GIRL GOES BAD
By **Adrienne**

THE COST OF LOYALTY 1-3
By **Kweli**

BRIDE OF A HUSTLA 1-3
THE FETTI GIRLS 1-3
CORRUPTED BY A GANGSTA 1-4
BLINDED BY HIS LOVE
THE PRICE YOU PAY FOR LOVE 1-3
DOPE GIRL MAGIC 1-3
By **Destiny Skai**

A KINGPIN'S AMBITION
A KINGPIN'S AMBITION II
I MURDER FOR THE DOUGH
By **Ambitious**

TRUE SAVAGE 1-7
DOPE BOY MAGIC 1-3
MIDNIGHT CARTEL 1-3
CITY OF KINGZ 1&2
NIGHTMARE ON SILENT AVE
THE PLUG OF LIL MEXICO 1&2
CLASSIC CITY
By **Chris Green**

A GANGSTER'S REVENGE 1-4
THE BOSS MAN'S DAUGHTERS 1-5
A SAVAGE LOVE 1&2
BAE BELONGS TO ME 1&2
A HUSTLER'S DECEIT 1-3
WHAT BAD BITCHES DO 1-3
SOUL OF A MONSTER 1-3
KILL ZONE
A DOPE BOY'S QUEEN 1-3
TIL DEATH 1-3
IMMA DIE BOUT MINE 1-6
DYING FOR LIKES
By **Aryanna**

A DOPEBOY'S PRAYER
By **Eddie "Wolf" Lee**

THE KING CARTEL 1-3
By **Frank Gresham**

THESE NIGGAS AIN'T LOYAL 1-3
By **Nikki Tee**

GANGSTA SHYT 1-3
By **CATO**

THE ULTIMATE BETRAYAL
By **Phoenix**

BOSS'N UP 1-3
By **Royal Nicole**

I LOVE YOU TO DEATH
By **Destiny J**

I RIDE FOR MY HITTA
I STILL RIDE FOR MY HITTA
By **Misty Holt**

LOVE & CHASIN' PAPER
By **Qay Crockett**

TO DIE IN VAIN
SINS OF A HUSTLA
By **ASAD**

BROOKLYN HUSTLAZ
By **Boogsy Morina**

BROOKLYN ON LOCK 1 & 2
By **Sonovia**

GANGSTA CITY
By **Teddy Duke**

A DRUG KING AND HIS DIAMOND 1-3
A DOPEMAN'S RICHES
HER MAN, MINE'S TOO 1&2
CASH MONEY HO'S
THE WIFEY I USED TO BE 1&2
PRETTY GIRLS DO NASTY THINGS
By **Nicole Goosby**

LIPSTICK KILLAH 1-3
CRIME OF PASSION 1-3
FRIEND OR FOE 1-3
By **Mimi**

TRAPHOUSE KING 1-3
KINGPIN KILLAZ 1-3
STREET KINGS 1&2
PAID IN BLOOD 1&2
CARTEL KILLAZ 1-3
DOPE GODS 1&2
By **Hood Rich**

THE STREETS ARE CALLING
By **Duquie Wilson**

STEADY MOBBN' 1-3
THE STREETS STAINED MY SOUL 1-3
By **Marcellus Allen**

WHO SHOT YA 1-3
SON OF A DOPE FIEND 1-4
HEAVEN GOT A GHETTO 1&2
SKI MASK MONEY 1&2
By **Renta**

GORILLAZ IN THE BAY 1-4
TEARS OF A GANGSTA 1/&2
3X KRAZY 1&2
STRAIGHT BEAST MODE 1&2
By **DE'KARI**

TRIGGADALE 1-3
MURDA WAS THE CASE 1-3
By **Elijah R. Freeman**

SLAUGHTER GANG 1-3
RUTHLESS HEART 1-3
By **Willie Slaughter**

GOD BLESS THE TRAPPERS 1-3
THESE SCANDALOUS STREETS 1-3
FEAR MY GANGSTA 1-5
THESE STREETS DON'T LOVE NOBODY 1-2
BURY ME A G 1-5
A GANGSTA'S EMPIRE 1-4
THE DOPEMAN'S BODYGAURD 1&2
THE REALEST KILLAZ 1-3
THE LAST OF THE OGS 1-3
By **Tranay Adams**

MARRIED TO A BOSS 1-3
By **Destiny Skai & Chris Green**

KINGZ OF THE GAME 1-7
CRIME BOSS 1-4
By **Playa Ray**

FUK SHYT
By **Blakk Diamond**

DON'T F#CK WITH MY HEART 1&2
By **Linnea**

ADDICTED TO THE DRAMA 1-3
IN THE ARM OF HIS BOSS
By **Jamila**

LOYALTY AIN'T PROMISED 1&2
By **Keith Williams**

YAYO 1-4
A SHOOTER'S AMBITION 1&2
BRED IN THE GAME
By **S. Allen**

TRAP GOD 1-3
RICH $AVAGE 1-3
MONEY IN THE GRAVE 1-3
CARTEL MONEY 1&2
By **Martell Troublesome Bolden**

FOREVER GANGSTA 1&2
GLOCKS ON SATIN SHEETS 1&2
By **Adrian Dulan**

TOE TAGZ 1-4
LEVELS TO THIS SHYT 1&2
IT'S JUST ME AND YOU
By **Ah'Million**

KINGPIN DREAMS 1-3
RAN OFF ON DA PLUG
By **Paper Boi Rari**

THE STREETS MADE ME 1-3
By **Larry D. Wright**

CONFESSIONS OF A GANGSTA 1-4
CONFESSIONS OF A JACKBOY 1-3
CONFESSIONS OF A HITMAN
CONFESSIONS OF A DOPE BOY
By **Nicholas Lock**

I'M NOTHING WITHOUT HIS LOVE
SINS OF A THUG
TO THE THUG I LOVED BEFORE
A GANGSTA SAVED XMAS
IN A HUSTLER I TRUST
By **Monet Dragun**

QUIET MONEY 1-3
THUG LIFE 1-3
EXTENDED CLIP 1&2
A GANGSTA'S PARADISE
By **Trai'Quan**

CAUGHT UP IN THE LIFE 1-3
THE STREETS NEVER LET GO 1-3
By **Robert Baptiste**

NEW TO THE GAME 1-3
MONEY, MURDER & MEMORIES 1-3
By **Malik D. Rice**

CREAM 2-3
THE STREETS WILL TALK
By **Yolanda Moore**

THE STREETS WILL NEVER CLOSE 1-3
By **K'ajji**

LIFE OF A SAVAGE 1-4
A GANGSTA'S QUR'AN 1-4
MURDA SEASON 1-3
GANGLAND CARTEL 1-3
CHI'RAQ GANGSTAS 1-4
KILLERS ON ELM STREET 1-3
JACK BOYZ N DA BRONX 1-3
A DOPEBOY'S DREAM 1-3
JACK BOYS VS DOPE BOYS 1-3
COKE GIRLZ
COKE BOYS
SOSA GANG 1&2
BRONX SAVAGES
BODYMORE KINGPINS
BLOOD OF A GOON
By **Romell Tukes**

CONCRETE KILLA 1-3
VICIOUS LOYALTY 1-3
BLOODY MONEY BAGS
By **Kingpen**

THE ULTIMATE SACRIFICE 1-6
KHADIFI
IF YOU CROSS ME ONCE 1-3
ANGEL 1-4
IN THE BLINK OF AN EYE
By **Anthony Fields**

THE LIFE OF A HOOD STAR
By **Ca$h & Rashia Wilson**

NIGHTMARES OF A HUSTLA 1-3
BLOOD AND GAMES 1&2
By **King Dream**

GHOST MOB
By **Stilloan Robinson**

HARD AND RUTHLESS 1&2
MOB TOWN 251
THE BILLIONAIRE BENTLEYS 1-3
REAL G'S MOVE IN SILENCE
By **Von Diesel**

MOB TIES 1-7
SOUL OF A HUSTLER, HEART OF A KILLER 1-3
GORILLAZ IN THE TRENCHES
OOPS CRY TOO 1&2
THE DAUGHTER OF A CARTEL BOSS
By **SayNoMore**

BODYMORE MURDERLAND 1-3
THE BIRTH OF A GANGSTER 1-4
By **Delmont Player**

FOR THE LOVE OF A BOSS 1&2
By **C. D. Blue**

KILLA KOUNTY 1-5
TENDER
By **Khufu**

MOBBED UP 1-4
THE BRICK MAN 1-5
THE COCAINE PRINCESS 1-10
STEPPERS 1-3
SUPER GREMLIN 1-4
A GANGSTA'S SON
By **King Rio**

MONEY GAME 1&2
By **Smoove Dolla**

A GANGSTA'S KARMA 1-5
By **FLAME**

KING OF THE TRENCHES 1-3
By **GHOST & TRANAY ADAMS**

BAD BITCHES WIT GUNZ 1&2
PROBLEM SOLVED
By "Christopher Diesel" Hornezes

QUEEN OF THE ZOO 1&2
By **Black Migo**

GRIMEY WAYS 1-3
BETRAYAL OF A G
By **Ray Vinci**

XMAS WITH AN ATL SHOOTER
By **Ca$h & Destiny Skai**

KING KILLA 1&2
By **Vincent "Vitto" Holloway**

BETRAYAL OF A THUG 1&2
By **Fre$h**

COUNTDOWN OF A KILLA 1&2
SEX, MURDER AND GOD 1&2
GUNS DOWN, BOTTOMS UP 1&2
By Lo-Life

THE MURDER QUEENS 1-7
By **Michael Gallon**

FOR THE LOVE OF BLOOD 1-4
By **Jamel Mitchell**

LAND OF THE HOOLIGANZ 4 | IRA B

HOOD CONSIGLIERE 1&2
NO TIME FOR ERROR
By **Keese**

PROTÉGÉ OF A LEGEND 1,2&3
LOVE IN THE TRENCHES 1&2
By **Corey Robinson**

THE PLUG'S RUTHLESS DAUGHTER 1&2
By **Tony Daniels**

BORN IN THE GRAVE 1-3
CRIME PAYS
By **Self Made Tay**

MOAN IN MY MOUTH
By **XTASY**

TORN BETWEEN A GANGSTER AND A GENTLEMAN
By **J-BLUNT & Miss Kim**

LOYALTY IS EVERYTHING 1-3
CITY OF SMOKE 1-3
By **Molotti**

HERE TODAY GONE TOMORROW 1&2
By **Fly Rock**

WOMEN LIE MEN LIE 1-4
FIFTY SHADES OF SNOW 1-3
STACK BEFORE YOU SPLURGE
GIRLS FALL LIKE DOMINOES
NAÏVE TO THE STREETS
By **ROY MILLIGAN**

PILLOW PRINCESS
By **S. Hawkins**

THE BUTTERFLY MAFIA 1-3
SALUTE MY SAVAGERY 1&2
By **Fumiya Payne**

THE LANE 1&2
By Ken-Ken Spence

THE PUSSY TRAP 1-5
By **Nene Capri**

DIRTY DNA
By **Blaque**

SANCTIFIED AND HORNY
by **XTASY**

BOOKS BY LDP'S CEO, CA$H

TRUST IN NO MAN
TRUST IN NO MAN 2
TRUST IN NO MAN 3
BONDED BY BLOOD
SHORTY GOT A THUG
THUGS CRY
THUGS CRY 2
THUGS CRY 3
TRUST NO BITCH
TRUST NO BITCH 2
TRUST NO BITCH 3
TIL MY CASKET DROPS
RESTRAINING ORDER
RESTRAINING ORDER 2
IN LOVE WITH A CONVICT
LIFE OF A HOOD STAR
XMAS WITH AN ATL SHOOTER